TURNS
OUT I'M AN
ALIEN

Turns Out I'm An Alien
An original concept by author Lou Treleaven
© Lou Treleaven

Cover artwork by James Lancett
Represented by The Bright Agency
www.thebrightagency.com

Published by MAVERICK ARTS PUBLISHING LTD
Studio 3a, City Business Centre, 6 Brighton Road,
Horsham, West Sussex, RH13 5BB
+44 (0) 1403 256941
© Maverick Arts Publishing Limited May 2019

A CIP catalogue record for this book is available
at the British Library.

ISBN: 978-1-84886-425-2

TURNS OUT I'M AN ALIEN

LOU TRELEAVEN

To Dad, and his sci-fi collection
which kept me enthralled

1

TURNS OUT
GREEN HAIR ISN'T NORMAL

I'm Jasper. I'm eleven years old and four foot six inches tall, with green eyes and green hair, and this year I found out something amazing about myself. Turns out…

Hang on. I think I'd better start at the beginning.

I did mention the green hair, didn't I? I guess I should start with that. In fact, we should really go way back, back to the very day I was born…

"Waaah!"

That's me, trying out my first word. Clever, aren't I? I can already say waaah. I've just popped out of my mum and a nurse is holding me up like the captain of the winning team holding up a trophy.

I'm looking around and I can see my mum lying there looking a bit drained (well, exhausted actually) and my dad staring at me in disbelief.

Good memory, haven't I? Actually I can't remember a thing about being born. No one can. I'm just imagining. My teacher, Mrs Pardew, says I've got a pretty good imagination so I'm probably right. No one who was there is around to tell me I'm wrong, anyway.

"It's a boy," the nurse says. "Congratulations."

"WAAAH!"

You think that's me again, don't you? Well it's not. That's my dad, and he's just noticed my hair's green.

When my dad recovers he says some pretty hurtful stuff, like, "My son is a freak."

I'm sure I've got that part right.

And then my mum pulls herself up to look at me and says, "Take him away!" like a queen sending someone off to be executed.

That was the last I ever saw of my real parents.

Luckily it wasn't long before I got some brand new ones. Foster parents, they were called, but I just thought of them as parents. They were called Mary and Bill Clarkson. In fact, they still are. And they are the nicest people on the whole earth.

I liked them because they were so predictable. Maybe it was because I'd had a strange start in life and no one knew much about me. I knew everything about Mary and Bill. I knew that Mary liked to start her day with a cup of tea and a crossword. I knew that Bill always had a to-do list where the first item was 'Write a to-do list'. I knew that every day they'd be there for me, because that's what they did – they were foster carers.

Then one day Mary and Bill got an award for long service and when they realised how long they'd been doing it they decided it was high time to stop. Holly, my foster sister, was worried we'd be kicked out but Mary and Bill said we were their last two kids and that made us special.

"So special no one wants us," Holly said, and

Mary said, "I'm not allowed to say this, but I'll say it anyway: *good*."

So me, Hols, Mary and Bill ended up like an ordinary family. They loved us like they were our real parents. They didn't even mind my green hair.

Things were a bit different at school.

Bogeybrain.

Snothair.

Vomhead.

And that was just the teachers. Only joking. No, these were some of the green-themed names I got called by the other kids. I really liked the names until I realised the other kids weren't bigging me up after all. They just didn't like my hair.

I knew Mary dyed her roots every month. She is secretly grey because she is old to be a mum. So I thought I could be secretly green. I got her hair dye out of the bathroom cabinet and tipped the whole lot over my head. It worked – in a way.

For the next month, my face was dyed Vibrant Rich Auburn For Stubborn Greys.

The kids at school had to think of a few new names for me after that. Traffic Light Head was one.

So now I wear hats. And underneath I have very, very short hair. But you can still see a tinge of green.

After they stopped being foster parents to anyone else, Mary and Bill decided to rent out one of the old kid's rooms for a bit of extra cash.

Which brings us to now. Saturday.

"You will be quiet when the new lodger comes, won't you?" Bill said. "They'll be sleeping right here." He pointed at the door I was zooming past on my skateboard. "So maybe you can skateboard downstairs instead?"

"Yes!" I was never allowed to skateboard downstairs. In fact I was never allowed to skateboard upstairs either. I just did. I liked the new lodger already.

I scrambled down the stairs and into the kitchen.

"Watch it!" Mary cried, as a piece of what looked

like spaghetti wriggled out of her hand and made a dash across the kitchen counter.

I tried to grab it. It thrashed about and shot out of my hands. Spaghetti didn't normally do that.

"I'd take that spaghetti back to the shop if I were you," I told Mary. "I think it's gone off."

Mary ignored me and plunged her hand into a jar. Inside, more stuff was wriggling.

"What *is* that?" I read the label on the jar. "Cosmic worms? Best stored in a vacuum?"

"Go and bother Holly for a bit," Mary said.

"But–"

"Now please, Jasper."

I left my skateboard and ran up to Holly's room. Some of my friends have big sisters and they're vile, always sulking and talking about boys and makeup, but Holly's not like that at all. Even though she's three years older than me, she's like my best friend.

"Hols?" I reached up to bang on the door, hitting the nose of boy band member and pop sensation, Harry Handsome. On a poster, not in real life

10

although that would have been even better. Harry Handsome was everywhere at the moment – not only on my sister's door but on the radio, the TV and even the side of buses. He had just split up with his boy band, This Way Up, and was apparently devastated. So devastated that he'd quickly recorded a solo album and was all over the charts with his new hit, 'I'm So Sensitive (You Wouldn't Believe It)' which I had already heard one million billion times coming from the depths of Holly's room.

Holly opened the door a crack. 'I'm So Sensitive (You Wouldn't Believe It)' blared out from her tinny speaker. "Don't touch my poster!" she snarled.

"But I was only–"

"And don't come in my room. Ever."

The door slammed. Maybe knocking in the middle of the song was the wrong thing to do. Oh well, it was easy to fix. I'd just wait till the end and quickly knock again before it restarted.

Just then Bill appeared from the attic stairs carrying a duster. "I thought you were skateboarding somewhere out of sight."

"Mary told me to go and bother Holly. But she doesn't want me around either." At least, not while Harry Handsome was on. "I only wanted to talk about the lodger."

"Ah." Bill looked serious. "Jasper, we'd rather you didn't talk about the lodger. With anyone."

"Wow. Who's coming? Some sort of criminal mastermind? Bill, you should hand them in to the police, you know that, don't you?"

Bill laughed. It wasn't a real laugh, just the right sort of noise. "What sort of people do you think we are? Honestly, Jasper, you do let your imagination run away with you sometimes."

"You sound like Mrs Pardew. I can meet them though, can't I?"

"They're arriving very late."

"I can stay up."

"As in, night time."

"Sleep is overrated. I've heard you say so yourself when you've got indigestion. And why–"

Bill waved the duster at me and walked off. I narrowed my eyes, partly because I was suspicious and partly because I had dust in them. Maybe Bill and Mary *were* harbouring a criminal mastermind. Maybe they weren't as ordinary and predictable as I'd always thought they were.

Interesting.

I needed to talk this over with someone. I banged on Holly's door. The song had ended. She'd be up for a chat now. She always was.

"Go away, bog breath!"

I stared at the poster of Harry Handsome until his ultra-white smile started to hurt my eyes. Everything was changing. Bands were splitting up, sisters were acting weird, and new people were coming to the house that I wasn't allowed to know about. But at least the last one was easy. Becoming a zombie would sort it, no problem.

That evening Mary and Bill were really busy.

Mary was cooking some sort of glowing green rock, while Bill kept going upstairs and coming back saying things like, "It's a nice clear night out there," and "No sign of them yet but maybe they're still orbiting." Then Bill asked Mary where his old bird-watching binoculars were and took them upstairs with him. Very interesting.

At nine o'clock, they told us both to go to bed.

"But–" I said.

"That's so unfair!" Holly said.

"Don't worry," I said to her as we went upstairs. "We can still meet up for midnight feasts when the lodger's here if that's what you're worried about."

She looked at me like I had three heads. Then she slammed the door. Again.

I looked at Harry Handsome. I was doing a lot of that recently, and not because I wanted to. He had to be getting a headache too after all that door slamming. Maybe that was why he looked a bit dim.

It seemed I was on my own. Time for the Jasper Plan. I dashed to my room, put my pyjamas on in case I was caught and had to pretend I was sleepwalking (easy: adopt zombie position with arms out and mumble nonsense), and grabbed my telescope. The ladder to the attic was pulled down. So that's where Bill was. I climbed up and pushed my way past boxes of old baby gear and a roll of carpet.

Bill was there, or rather, his legs were. He was standing on a chair with the top bit of him poking out of a hatch in the roof I'd never noticed before. "Black Hole roundabout," he was murmuring. "Yes, that must be it. Always hold ups around the Black Hole roundabout."

I lifted my telescope to my eye. Instantly I could see vibrant colours moving in and out of each other and forming amazing patterns. Wow! Outer space was mind-blowing! Then I realised it wasn't a telescope. I was looking through my kaleidoscope instead.

"Who's there?" Bill asked, before he fell off his chair onto the floor.

"Giant laughing tomatoes are chasing me!" I mumbled randomly, lifting my arms into zombie position, but I stopped as someone else fell through the hatch and on top of Bill.

The someone else looked more like a some*thing* else. It was large and round but only about half Bill's height, with bright orange skin. For a minute I thought my space hopper, which had burst five years ago when Bill sat on it, had been miraculously reinflated and given the gift of life.

"Appalling," it said in a posh English accent. "Those space taxis have no idea about customer service." It brushed itself down with tiny arms. "I booked a controlled descent with cushioned landing. The only cushion was my oversized orange behind. Bill, you old codger! How many years has it been? A lot, by the look of you. I'm ageless, naturally."

Bill laughed and then he and the alien did some sort of complicated handshake. I gawped. Then it turned towards me.

"Ah, so this is the youngster. Greetings from Snood. That's my home planet by the way, not some random oddly-named person I'm passing on a message for. Although I do do that sometimes."

"What?" My first word to an alien was 'what'. Now it wouldn't even know I was an intelligent life form. The fact was, I had nothing to say. I was, for the first time ever, completely empty of every thought but the one telling me there was an alien in front of me. I had to get it out. "Bill? Bill! There's an alien in front of me."

Bill scrambled to his feet. "Yes. Now listen, Jasper. You haven't seen anything, okay?"

"Haven't seen anything? Are you trying to hypnotise me or something? I am seeing something and it's an alien!"

"You called him Jasper, eh? Fascinating." The alien looked me up and down. It wore a long apron and not much else. Luckily the long apron hid anything that might have been embarrassing.

"And you haven't seen anything either, Flarp,"

Bill said pointedly.

"Flarp?" I repeated.

The alien gave a little bow. "Flarp Moonchaser, Slayer of the Multi-Headed Muck Monster of Murg, and retired customer service executive at the Galactic Tourist Office. The Muck Monster thing was a complete accident, by the way, but it sounds good." Flarp held out its hand. "I believe this is what you do for a greeting in this particular zone of Earth?"

I paused. An alien hand was reaching towards me. This was quite a big deal.

"I'm not going to vaporise you, you know."

I laughed nervously and stretched out my hand.

"At least, not while I haven't got my vaporiser charged up. I'm joking! There." Flarp pumped my hand up and down. It felt just like I'd been expecting. Like shaking hands with a space hopper.

"Is that your bag?" I asked, pointing to a spiny sphere with a handle.

"Goodness, yes. You'll have to be quick, it's

programmed to repel strangers," Flarp called as it began to roll away.

"No, Jasper! Don't touch anything!" Bill said.

It was the first time I'd ever been asked to do something by an alien and Bill was telling me not to? Like that was going to happen. I made a dive and grabbed at some spines. The sphere fell into two parts and things began to tumble out, things I'd never seen before and didn't have names for, like a glowing ball with stars floating in it, a long stretchy thing with buttons that beeped and a book called 'Take it Easy on Earth – all you need to know to retire on the Third Planet'. At least I had a name for that. It was a book, wasn't it? Until it opened and projected a massive picture of the earth on the wall.

"If you like breathing in oxygen and breathing out carbon dioxide – and, let's face it, who doesn't? – Earth is the perfect planet on which to retire," began a piercingly loud American voice. "The average IQ is exceptionally low for a carbon-based life form, meaning you should be able to live out a peaceful existence with no unwelcome disturbances or autopsies to bother you–"

"The end," Bill said firmly. The book closed and the picture disappeared. Meanwhile the long stretchy thing had stuck to my slipper and wouldn't let go.

"Bill? Help."

"I told you, Jasper." He pulled it off with a *schlup* and stuffed it into the strange bag with the other things. "Why don't you go to bed while I take our visitor down to the kitchen for some cosmic worms – I mean, a perfectly ordinary cup of tea?"

Flarp was looking at me with interest again. "You are a spoilsport, Bill. I'm sure Jasper would love to join us–"

"I know. That's the trouble," Bill said quickly. "This way, old friend. You haven't told me about the rest of your flight. Did you get the complimentary inflatable toothbrush? I always find them a tad bendy in the middle…"

Their voices disappeared as they went downstairs

together.

"Well," I said to myself, stunned. Not least by Bill's impressive handshake manoeuvre which I was determined to learn and replicate with my friends at the earliest opportunity.

"Well," echoed a familiar voice behind me.

I looked round and there were Holly's legs. Luckily they were attached to the rest of her. She was on the chair and peering out of the hatch.

"This thing's rubbish," she said, waving my telescope at me. So that's where it was. "All I could make out was the word 'taxi'."

"You saw a taxi?"

"I saw a UFO, barf brain." She climbed down. "I think there's something Mary and Bill aren't telling us."

"There's a lot Mary and Bill aren't telling us. Like, did you know Bill can do this handshake that looks like he's double-jointed or something?"

Holly gave me a playful shove. "Come on, worm. Let's go and find out."

2
TURNS OUT MARY AND BILL AREN'T WHO THEY SEEM (I WAS RIGHT)

Holly and I crept down to the kitchen. It was just like old times, getting food for midnight feasts, except for an alien being in the house and Harry Handsome staring out of Holly's t-shirt with 'broody eyes'. And the weird sounds pulsing out around the kitchen door.

The music surged as Holly pushed the door open. The kitchen table was shoved back and Mary was boogying with the alien. Bill was pouring foaming cocktails and wiggling his hips. The music was like nothing I'd ever heard. In fact I wasn't even sure it was music, more like rhythmic farting to the accompaniment of someone emptying a bin, but

Mary seemed to be enjoying it.

I stared open-mouthed until dribble started to go down my chin.

Holly, as usual, was more direct. "Mary? Bill? What do you think you're doing?"

"Oh – er, hi kids," Mary said, stopping mid-pogo.

Bill flicked a switch. The music stopped and my ears wept with relief. "I thought I told you to go to bed?" he said.

Holly crossed her arms firmly. "Why is Mary doing the twist with an alien? Why aren't you falling asleep in front of the TV with a to-do list in your lap? What's wrong with you both?"

"Flarp, this is Holly," Mary said. "And I believe you've met Jasper."

"Greetings from the four corners of the universe," Flarp said, making little corner signs with its hands. "Most people think that's a figure of speech, by the way, but the universe really does have four corners. Well, I suppose they're more like folds really. Well, when I say folds, they could probably be more accurately described as pleats–"

Holly stepped forward. "What's going on?"

Mary took her hands. "Sweetheart, I'm sorry. This is a whole different part of our lives that we weren't ready to share with you yet. But maybe we should. Bill?"

"Gotcha. Three Nebulian Chin Slammers coming right up," Bill said, busying himself at the counter.

"Better make that five," Mary said. "It could be a long night."

"We're going to drink Nebulian Chin Slammers?" I didn't know what they were but they sounded dangerously grown-up and exciting.

"No, Jasper. You two can have Auntie Tentacle's Fungoo Squash. Those extra drinks are for me. I've got a lot to tell you."

The kitchen table was resituated and we all sat round while Bill gave me and Holly a short, fat glass each, full of rubbery brown stuff too thick to drink. I didn't mind though as I was sitting next to Flarp.

A real-life alien! I kept sneaking glimpses at it. Strangely, it also kept sneaking glimpses at me.

"What's this again?"

"Auntie Tentacle's Fungoo Squash. It's a popular children's drink on Snood. Flarp brought it."

"They're trying to poison us," Holly said, pushing hers away.

I took a sip. It was… rubbery. I attempted a chew.

Mary sipped her cocktail. "I first met Bill on Uranus."

I stopped chewing and sniggered.

"Jasper, please listen properly."

"I am."

Mary gave me her 'be quiet or else' look. "I'd gone to Uranus as a guest member of the Seventh Planet Re-Branding Committee while Bill was hiking across the famous mountain range, Twin Cheeks."

It was too much for me. I spat a mouthful of Fungoo across the room where it bounced a few times before coming to rest in a far corner. Mary decided to ignore me.

"Oh yes, I was quite involved in solar system politics in my day. But three weeks of sitting around discussing whether Uranus should be renamed 'Posterior', 'Behind' or simply 'Butt' was getting to me. When I saw Bill stuck in the cleft of Twin Cheeks I realised what was really important in life. I rescued him and we took the next shuttle back to Earth, got married and started our wonderful foster family. Stop snorting, Jasper."

"So what are you saying? Bill's an alien?" Holly asked.

"That explains a lot," I said, getting up to chase my blob of Fungoo across the floor and giving up.

"Don't be ridiculous, Holly," Mary said. "Of course Bill isn't an alien – whatever next? No, he's an escaped prisoner on the run from the Andromedans."

"Very good, Mary. I nearly believed all of it." Holly stood up, leaving her Fungoo untouched. A good idea – I wished I'd never started mine. "I'm off to bed before this gets any weirder. I'll see you in the morning. Nice alien costume by the way – not. I recognised Jasper's old space hopper a mile off."

We watched Holly leave in silence. I hate silence. "How come you never told us all this before?"

"Would you have believed us if we had?"

Mary was right. I would have thought she was off her rocker if she'd started going on about Bill being stuck in a cleft in Uranus. But because of what had already happened today, it now seemed almost normal.

"So where else have you been, then?"

Mary counted on her fingers. "The Proxima Centauri system, of course. Betelgeuse – overrated, I thought. Trappist-1 was a lot of fun, though, wasn't it Bill?"

Bill nodded vigorously as he sipped his cocktail. A bit of green smoke came out of his ears.

I attempted another slurp of Fungoo and instantly regretted it. "So why is nobody else zipping around going to different planets, then? How come you got to do it?"

Mary looked a bit guilty. "I shouldn't have really. It was all a big accident. When I was a teenager I found an abandoned spaceship and stupidly climbed into it."

Flarp put up a stubby hand. "Guilty. One of my testing pods. Should have picked them all up after my last visit."

"I leaned on the autopilot and it whisked me off to the planet Snood in the Outer Headmashup Partriculon," Mary said. At least I think that's what she said. "I met Flarp there and she trained me in everything she knew."

"She?" I repeated.

"We have a range of genders on Snood," Flarp explained. "Female is probably the closest Earth equivalent. That or mushroom."

"What?"

Mary clapped a hand on the alien's back. "All you need to know is, this is Flarp Moonchaser, Slayer of the Multi-Headed Muck Monster of Murg, and all-round space hero."

"Oh, tish. I'm retired now," Flarp said. "And the Muck Monster really was an accident. I'm surprised it didn't sue me, actually. Mind you, it was dead which makes that sort of thing a tad challenging. No, these days I just pootle around the local galaxy cluster looking up old pals. Like these two reprobates."

"So did Flarp train Bill as well?" I asked.

Mary shook her head. "Bill was abducted from Earth by the Andromedans as a child and grew up in one of their prison camps."

Poor Bill. Stuck in a butt cleft, and now this.

Bill put down his glass and took over the story. "I fell asleep in the middle of a crop circle. It was my own fault, really. After ten years in the Andromedan prison, I managed to escape by stowing away in an interstellar pirate ship. I soon proved myself a useful crew member and was able to work my passage back to the solar system. I said passage back, not back passage, Jasper! Honestly, you're obsessed. Anyway, I'd got as far as Uranus when I met Mary and we travelled the rest of the way together. We learned a valuable lesson."

"There's no place like Earth?"

"No." Bill drained his glass. "Always barter with services rather than goods. And the best place for fake passports is Ten-Eye Twistifoot's Identity Emporium near Betelgeuse."

Mary chuckled. "Do you remember, Flarp, when you got caught in that time-space-dimension loop on Globula IV?"

"And became my own great-grandmother?" Flarp laughed heartily. It sounded a bit like a balloon deflating. "Good times. I know, how about we move on to Nurishan Knee Jerkers?"

"Are you sure?" Bill eyed Mary. "We all know where those lead, don't we?"

Mary pretended to sniff haughtily. "Just because I danced on the holo-bar with the Centauri Ambassador doesn't mean I can't take my drink."

"Wait!" I pulled at Mary's arm. "I still don't

understand why you didn't tell us any of this before."

"Jasper, our days as space-faring adventurers are well and truly over," Bill said as he poured a frothy liquid into Flarp's glass. It spiralled around the bottom like a tiny galaxy. "And the Andromedans are still looking for me – they have spies everywhere. We want to keep our past to ourselves. And Mary doesn't want any more episodes like the one with the Centauri Ambassador."

"Not at my age anyway," Mary put in.

"We are happy to put up Flarp as an old friend but we don't want to get involved anymore, and we certainly don't want the whole world descending on Little Blanding to gawp at her which is why you must not tell anyone."

I stared at them as the enormity of what they had just asked me sunk in. I mean, it was fair enough asking me not to talk about a lodger, but an alien?

"Anyone?" I queried.

"Anyone."

"Not even Chad, Max, Charlie, Ali and Jake?" I reeled off the names of my five best friends. Surely it would be okay to tell them?

"*Especially* not Chad, Max, Charlie, Ali and Jake," Mary said, looking at me sternly over the top of her glass.

"But I'll burst."

"Good, then you definitely won't be able to tell anyone. Goodnight, Jasper."

"But–"

Mary turned away. Bill lifted his glass to me, then started telling an anecdote about getting lost while looking for the toilet in Flim-Blub's Flubber Club on Jondle XI and almost walking into a dark matter accelerator. I longed to interrupt, but every time I opened my mouth they just gestured at me to shut up. Eventually I got the message and trudged out. I needed to talk to someone – to anyone. Then I remembered who was always up for a chat – Holly! I raced upstairs and came face to face with her closed door. On it, half-covering the slightly less handsome half of Harry Handsome's face, was a hand-written sign saying 'Push off Jasper'.

"But–" I protested through the door.

"I said push off!" Holly yelled.

I walked back to my room. My walls were covered in posters from my favourite film – Cosmos Wars. I lay on my bed and stared at them, imagining Mary and Bill going into space. Mary and Bill driving spaceships and diving about avoiding attacking aliens. It was just too incredible to be true. Maybe I'd wake up and it would all be a dream.

So that's what I tried.

The next morning was Sunday, but I got up early anyway and ran downstairs. Mary was drinking a cup of tea and doing the crossword. Bill was writing a to-do list with 'Write a to-do list' as the first item.

"What's wrong?" Mary asked, staring at me.

"Nothing. Just thought I'd get up early, that's all."

"But it's Sunday. Bill, feel his forehead."

"I'm fine."

"Then why are you staring at us like that?"

I dragged my eyes away and poured myself a bowl of breakfast hoops. There was nothing weird in the cereal cupboard. Mary and Bill were doing normal things. Perhaps yesterday had been a crazy dream. Maybe I was working too hard at school. Yes, that was it. I'd always told Mrs Pardew homework was bad for me.

"So what's happening today?" I asked.

Mary shrugged. "I thought I'd read the paper and potter about the garden."

"And I'll tackle this list," Bill said. "Starting with changing the light bulb in the living room."

I was yawning already. Mary and Bill were back to their ordinary selves. Everything was normal again. It had all been a dream. I supposed that was a good thing, really. I mean, aliens in Little Blanding? It just couldn't happen.

"Actually, I think I'll take this back to bed," I said, grabbing my cereal bowl and a spoon and leaving them to it.

I'd just closed my bedroom door and started tucking in when Holly burst in.

"Oh my god, they've been lying to us for years!" she squealed, jumping on my bed and sending half my hoops flying into the air.

I scooched up and rescued what I could. "Who?"

"Mary and Bill of course!"

"I thought you didn't believe them."

"I didn't, until I found this in the recyc." Holly smoothed out a crumpled piece of paper.

Dear Mrs Mary Clarkson,

As a citizen of the Milky Way, you are invited to vote at the Galactic Local Group Annual General Meeting on Flumbleplank 1400000X25 B, or 19 September in your Earth calendar. Please let us know in advance of any dietary or respiratory requirements. Your portal is the self-service checkout at your local Asbi's supermarket which will be active between ⊖ and ⯑, or 1900 and 1915 in your Earth hours.

May the slime of eternity course through your veins with ill-disguised zeal.

Yours unyieldingly,

Iko Iko Iko,

Son of Iko Iko,

Grandson of Iko,

Emperor of Andromeda (and lots of other places as well).

"They told us lying was wrong," Holly said, throwing the letter down on the bed.

"You don't have to lie, just don't tell anyone."

"No, I mean they've lied to us. They've always lied to us. They wouldn't even have told us last night if we hadn't gone down and found them partying in the kitchen."

I picked up the letter.

"I bet they didn't even say anything about it this morning either," Holly continued. "Did they?"

Maybe Holly was right. Maybe Mary and Bill didn't trust us. Maybe it was because we weren't their real children, just kids they were hanging on to because no one else wanted them.

"No," I admitted.

"You see?" Holly said. "They're liars. About everything. Don't you see what that means? No matter how much they say they want to keep us, they don't. Not really."

"Your eyeliner's running," I pointed out. But she had already slammed the door.

She was even slamming *my* door now.

I wasn't sure I believed Holly about Mary and Bill not wanting us. But something else was worrying me. If they had had such a good time in space, why didn't they want to go back? Maybe they secretly did – and they'd have an even better time without two kids around. Then we'd have to go to another foster home. And I didn't want to go to another foster home. I wanted to stay here forever.

I read the letter again. It was totally confusing. Everything was confusing. I needed help. And there was only one person I could think of who could give me some answers.

Flarp Moonchaser, Slayer of the Multi-Headed Muck Monster of Murg and all-round space hero. I shoved Mary's invite in my pocket and headed for the guest room.

3

TURNS OUT I'M... WELL, YOU'VE PROBABLY GUESSED BY NOW

Visiting our visitor was not as easy as I had expected. As I headed purposefully towards the guest room, Bill cut me off and told me to pop down to Asbi's because we were running out of milk. When I got back he told me he was really sorry, but we were also running out of bread and I'd have to go back. When I got back from *that*, he suddenly remembered we were also out of teabags, butter and cat food. We don't even have a cat.

"I know what you're doing," I told Bill after the fourth trip, but he pretended he didn't hear me and sent me off to pressure wash the bin. By the end of the day I was exhausted.

Before I knew it, it was Monday and school again. I couldn't concentrate and spent all day drawing aliens zapping each other in my exercise book. It was exactly what I did all day anyway so Mrs Pardew didn't notice any difference. At home, Holly stayed in her room mooning over Harry Handsome, while I played football in Little Blanding Park with Chad, Max, Charlie, Ali and Jake. But all they talked about was what was happening at school and who was on telly last night. Suddenly all that didn't seem so interesting anymore when there were real life aliens around.

"So what's happening with you, Jasper?"

"Nothing."

"Nothing?"

"Well, Bill changed a light bulb."

It was torture.

I was on a quest. A quest for answers. What was this letter, and why was everything such a secret? While Mary was busy chasing spaghetti round the kitchen again, I went up to the lodger's room.

On the door was a Do Not Disturb sign in five alien languages. At least, I guessed they were alien and I guessed what they said. I ignored all of them and pushed the door open.

The last resident in this room had been Sam, the messiest foster brother I had ever had. Our new guest made Sam look like a tidiness freak. The surfaces were covered with strange alien artefacts that were either throbbing, beeping or pulsing. Some were doing all three. There were odd statues, twisted rocks and bits of metal. I wanted to touch everything.

"Go on," Flarp said, waving at me. "Touch everything. I would if I were you."

I touched a flashing metal box. It opened up into a map the size of a duvet cover with coloured planets and dots moving between them.

"Mmm. Interesting you should pick that," Flarp said. "Civil unrest in Andromeda. Bill went there, you know."

"So it's true?" I asked.

"You poor life form. I see you know everything. I told Bill he couldn't keep it from you forever. I suppose you've come to me for the details? Very wise. Take a seat."

I looked around for an empty space but there wasn't one. I sat on the bed.

"Ah, so that's what it's for!" Flarp threw up her hands in delight. "I thought it was some sort of linen-flattening device." She joined me with an enthusiastic bounce. "Bill was terribly brave, you know. He couldn't bear to escape from that terrible Andromedan prison and leave you behind, not when you were just a tiny helpless baby. He knocked out a guard – not easy when they've got three heads – and stole a ship. He'd never flown an anti-matter powered space vehicle before but there's a first time for everything and Bill, let me tell you, was a natural. The journey home wasn't easy, mind you. He had a fleet of five hundred Andromedans on his tail, and to top it all off, you were teething–"

"Hang on." I had a sudden urge to aim a remote

at Flarp and rewind. "*Me?* Bill rescued *me?*"

"He had to. The Andromedans had you in this teeny tiny cell with no toys and an iron nappy–"

"I was on *Andromeda?*"

"*In* Andromeda. Andromeda is a galaxy – a collection of solar systems. Like your Milky Way but bigger. You were on one of their prison planets. They have many, unfortunately. Luckily you and Bill were on the same one. Anyway, let's get back to the exciting bit. Bill had almost made it back to the Milky Way when the Andromedan's front squadron dived on him. It was at that very moment that you said your very first word: 'Swerve right!' Technically that's two words, but–"

"I was in *prison?*"

Flarp stopped. "Exactly how much of this did you not know?"

"All of it. So I was rescued from a *prison* on *Andromeda?*"

Neither of us had noticed Mary come in. "Jasper! What are you doing, bothering Flarp when she's trying to work?"

"I'm retired," Flarp said.

"I was rescued from a *prison* on *Andromeda?*"
I repeated, stuck in a loop.

"Ah," Mary said. "He knows."

Flarp slid off the bed. "Oh dear. I'm so sorry,
Mary. When he came here asking questions, I
thought he knew he was an alien."

"I'm an *alien?*" I stood up, feeling dizzy. "I'm
an alien?"

"What's going on? I can't hear a single one of
Harry Handsome's brilliantly crafted and sensitive
song lyrics," Holly complained, pushing past Mary.

"Nothing," Mary said. "Nothing's going on."

"I'm an alien," I said.

Holly guffawed. "I could have told you that years
ago."

Mary stared at her. "*You* knew?"

"Knew what?" Bill said, squeezing in the
doorway.

"I'm an alien," I said. "You rescued me from

Andromeda."

Bill raised his eyebrows at Mary, took a deep breath and turned to me. "Yes," he said. "Yes, you are. You were kidnapped from your home in the Triangulum Galaxy and I rescued you. It was too dangerous for you to go back. It still is. You're safe here, where nobody knows who you are."

"The *Triangulum* Galaxy?" I said, my voice rising into a squeak. "Look, could everyone stop revealing new information just for one second?"

For the first time, no one spoke.

"Thank you."

"As a royal baby, you really should have been better looked after–" Flarp began.

"I'm *royal?* I can't take any more! I can't believe *no one* told me I'm an alien!" I pushed past them all and ran out, grabbing my coat and bobble hat on the way. I didn't know where I was going, just that I needed to be alone.

Alone with my royal, Triangulum, Andromedan prison-busting, alien self.

4
TURNS OUT THERE'S SOME SORT OF AN ALIEN CONFERENCE GOING ON

My alien self and I ran off to the park. I had no plan. It was just the only place I was allowed to go on my own. It was getting dark. My friends had gone home hours ago, for tea and telly. Suddenly I wished I was one of them – just an ordinary kid.

But I wasn't ordinary. I wasn't even a kid, because kids are human. Unless they're the goat kind. I wasn't even a goat. Goats come from Earth. I was an alien.

I sat on a swing and held the chains with my alien hands. I kicked my alien legs until the swing moved to and fro. What was in there, under my alien skin? Did I have two hearts? Five kidneys? An extra brain? Actually, I could probably rule that one out. I felt so normal. How could I be an alien? Everything about me was totally boring. Except...

My hair! Maybe that was my alien heritage. Plus there was my strange and embarrassing middle name. And maybe the other stuff was still to come. I hadn't finished growing yet. Maybe I'd get the urge to be alone, and go off and build a cocoon and come out as a monster. Maybe that was what was happening right now. No, I didn't feel the urge to build a cocoon. Phew. But maybe I'd grow a tail one day, or even wings. Anything could happen.

I jumped off the swing and clambered up the slope of the big slide until I stood at the top. I stared up into the darkened sky, and as I looked the first star popped out.

I was an alien. I came from somewhere up there. Mary and Bill had known all along. They were space adventurers. Bill had even rescued me from Andromeda! Why hadn't they told me? There was so much I needed to know, but Mary and Bill were the last people I wanted to talk to right now. I wanted to find things out myself – but how?

I shoved my hands in my pockets, and proved correct my theory that you can never wear the same pair of jeans for too long, as my hand miraculously found the crumpled invitation Holly had found in the recycling, the one I had been planning to show Flarp. I read it again. An alien meeting? 19 September? That was tonight! But what was all the stuff about the self-service checkout at Asbi's?

I looked across the road where the bright orange Asbi's sign blared, dazzling passers-by with its promise of cheap food and a central aisle of strange items no one ever needed like inflatable TVs and chip thermometers. It didn't take much imagination to think it might have been placed there by aliens who had no idea about human needs.

I stuffed the invite back in my pocket and slid down the slide. It felt wrong at night with no one else there, but I was an alien now. I could do odd things like that. I checked about to see that nobody

48

was around who might recognise me and ask me what I was up to, like our neighbours who liked to 'keep an eye' on me just because I'd once got stuck on their shed roof. Then I hurried over the road towards the shop.

I had been in Asbi's many times to get bits for Mary and Bill but this time felt different, partly because I didn't want to see anyone I knew and partly because it was my first time out in public as an alien. Was that man staring at me as he got his trolley? Why was that baby crying? Was I freaking her out with my cosmic vibes? I checked my reflection in the shop window. I still looked like me, but maybe that wasn't enough anymore. I made a special effort to look as human as possible. It's more difficult than you might think. I gave up and went inside.

The self-service checkout was at the front of the shop near the entrance, but I couldn't check out the checkout as there were loads of people waiting to check out and they were in the way. I had no choice but to join the end of a long queue. Everything seemed to be completely normal. I had another look at the invitation. It said the checkout would be active, whatever that meant, between 1900 and 1915. That meant seven to quarter past. It wasn't quite seven o'clock yet. Maybe at seven something weird would happen. But what? I craned round the woman in front of me, trying to get another peek. She turned round and looked me up and down.

"Waiting for someone, are you?"

Whoops. I had no shopping. I slapped my head as though I'd just remembered something and hurried off down the nearest aisle. I rummaged through some glow-in-the-dark pillow cases, a garden hammock and some boxes of chocolate teaspoons. Bingo. Edible cutlery – what was not to like? I scurried back to the self-service queue. It seemed to have doubled. Aargh! My watch was just about to tick over to seven. First I had been too early, and now I was going to be too late.

I tapped the shoulder of the person in front of me.

"Can I go before you? It's just, this happens to be an alien portal and I'm going to miss my slot."

Before the person in front could begin to frame a reply, a familiar robotic voice interrupted us.

"Unexpected item in bagging area."

No. Please. I couldn't miss this chance. I was at risk of bursting, and alien bits of me were about to go everywhere.

"Unexpected item in bagging area."

"It's saying there's an unexpected item in the bagging area," the cashier said, wandering over.

"Yeah, I got that," the man at the front said, shaking his head.

"Unexpected item in bagging area."

I checked my watch. Gone seven o'clock. Maybe this was it. It had to be it. The machine was going wrong because it was about to become an alien portal. My heart was thumping hard as I pushed my way to the front. Time for a masterclass from the Jasper School of Acting.

"Erm, hi. I think I can help."

The cashier and the man both looked at me in disbelief.

"Unexpected item in bagging area."

"Yeah, we – er – studied this at school. In design and technology. Let me have a look for you…" I reached past them and started patting the machine all over, looking for some sort of… well, I didn't know what. But there had to be something. This was an alien artefact, and I was an alien. If anyone could work out how to use it, it ought to be me. I started pulling off some panels.

"Unexpected item in bagging area."

The cashier was giving me a funny look. She backed away until she reached a small microphone by her till. "Manager to self-service checkout. Vandalism in progress. That's vandalism in progress."

"I'm not vandalising it, I'm trying to help!" I cried desperately. "I just need to consult my – er – revision notes."

The man who had been trying to use the

checkout abandoned his shopping and walked out. The other people in the queue, which was now pretty long, were starting to get hostile too. "Get out!" was shouted a few times, and even, "What planet is he on?" which I thought was a good one.

It was getting more embarrassing by the second as I saw what had to be the manager striding down the aisle towards me with an expression of righteous anger mixed with a tinge of excitement that something unexpected was happening on her shift. I quickly scanned the invitation one more time, hoping desperately for some sort of extra clue about what it meant. All it said was that the portal was the self-service checkout at Asbi's. There was nothing about how to use it.

And then I saw something. A tiny bar code embedded in the Andromedan coat of arms at the top.

"What's going on?" demanded the manager. "Oh, it's you. The one who's always buying one thing at a time."

"That was just one day–" I interrupted.

"If you don't leave, I'm calling security."

"It's all right. I am leaving." I gave her a big smile, hiding my real expression which was doubt mixed with a tinge of satisfaction, liberally coated with grated terror. Then I swiped the bar code.

"BEEP! Please place yourself in the bagging area," commanded the machine.

It was happening.

"What?" said the manager.

"Please place yourself in the bagging area."

I plonked my bottom on the metal plate. The manager opened her mouth to say something, the cashier raised an eyebrow and started to look vaguely interested, and then Asbi's and everything in it disappeared in a wibbly blur.

I don't know if you've ever teleported before but it's not very pleasant. One, it makes you feel sick, and two, all the molecules that make up your body are pulled out of place, whizz through the air and land somewhere completely different before reassembling themselves. Yes, that's how it happens. And the more you think about how it happens, the sicker it makes you feel. "Hyperspace is filled with vomit" as Flarp says, and I reckon most of it is mine.

Anyway, I didn't know this at the time. All I knew was that I was heaving and retching for a bit before I could work out where I was. But after I could finally stand up straight I was able to look around.

I was in a large circular hall with silver walls and a glass domed ceiling showing the stars. Around the edge were more windows and I could see a beautiful blue and white swirly planet out of one of them. It was Earth, wasn't it? Wow, that was weird and nearly made me feel sick again. I was in space! Actually in space! Once I'd got my head round this, I turned my attention back to the room.

Tiers of benches lined the walls and cascaded down to a central stage. The benches weren't attached to anything, as far as I could work out. They just floated. Oh, and one other thing I noticed. Yep, the whole place was filled with aliens. Big aliens, small aliens, aliens with three heads, aliens made of gas travelling about in little bubbles, aliens with no eyes, aliens with rows of little feet like toothbrush bristles… It was blowing my mind.

There was also lots of noise. Strange, alien squeaks and clurps. Yes, clurps. There were also beeps, twizzles and blups. These had to be alien languages. Either that or I was getting another one of my countless ear infections.

"Hi, how are you? I hope you had a pleasant trip. Yes? Awesome! Welcome to the conference. Here's your welcome pack," said a perky voice, thrusting a little cube into my hands. I stared at the creature in front of me – my second ever alien! This one was completely different to Flarp. It looked like a large fly without wings. Or maybe a really big raisin. It had a tray on a cord around its neck filled with little bags. It was like a giant raisin selling ice creams.

At this point, I seriously considered that I might be dreaming. Or unconscious. Maybe, to stop me vandalising the self-service checkout, the manager at Asbi's had knocked me out with a catering-sized tin of beans.

"What is it?" I asked, looking at the little cube the alien had just given me.

"Well, let's see now." It grabbed the box back and ripped it open. Before I could agree or preferably disagree it had started attaching things to me.

"This goes in here and this goes in here," it said, stuffing something in my ear and something else in my mouth.

"Omfnurrgah," I said. It was all I could manage with an alien hand in my mouth.

Luckily the alien seemed to understand me. "It's a GarbleGadget III, of course. Means you can speak and understand every language in the Local Group. Well, every language except Parpoid. They talk using the other end, if you know what I mean. Comfortable? Awesome!"

Actually, it was. Whatever the alien had put into me had now either disappeared or sunk into me somehow, because I couldn't feel it at all anymore. I could, however, suddenly hear lots of voices around me. Gone were the squeaks and clurps. Now there were real words. The accents were odd but I could get the gist of some of the comments, which mostly seemed to be about traffic problems in the Horsehead Nebula causing a ten light year tailback and a diversion around Orion's Belt.

"Wow. Thanks."

I was about to bombard the alien with questions when I felt something reptilian grab my shoulder. I turned round to see a large angry lizard in an uncomfortably tight suit complete with bow tie.

"Are you going to stand there all day? Take this flibberslurp to seat delta ten and be quick about it!" it said, shoving a tray of foaming bowls into my hands.

I stared at them, fascinated, as they popped and fizzled, sending little puffs of steam into the air which made me cough.

"Stop gawping and get serving or I'll put you on Parpoid toilet duty. And just so you know, Parpoids have seven butts. That way, idiot!"

The lizard creature grabbed me again, twisted me round by the shoulders and pushed me towards some stairs which led down between the rows of floating seats.

"Over here!" squeaked various thirsty aliens.

I headed towards them. Somehow, I had become a waiter. Every time my tray was empty, Lizard-face swiped it off me and thrust a full one into my hands. Before I knew it, I had served six different aliens with twelve different types of snacks and/or drinks (sometimes it was hard to tell). It wasn't what I had expected to be doing, but at least no one was asking me what I was doing there. Hey, maybe I would even get paid! I passed a small bottle of coloured gas to a thin beaker-shaped creature, who burped with thanks.

Suddenly an out-of-tune fanfare sounded and everyone scrambled to their feet – except the ones who didn't have feet, who hovered, floated or reared up, depending on the number of their limbs. Two tall, thin alien guards with purple uniforms and faces marched in, each holding a pole and a big impressive-looking ray gun thing. Hanging between the poles on a large hammock was a huge prickly purple ball with stubby arms and legs and a cross face. It was easily the biggest thing in the room.

"All hail Iko Iko Iko," said one of the guards.

"Son of Iko Iko…" said the other.

"Grandson of Iko…" said the first.

"Emperor of Andromeda Galaxy," said the other one.

"And a lot of other places too," finished the first one. "May his reign be long and full of terror and scary stuff."

The Emperor's hand, which had seemed very small, shot out like a lizard's tongue and hit the guard who had spoken in the face. "Enough! We are here to vote on whether the great and all conquering galaxy of Andromeda, of which I am Emperor–"

"All hail the Emperor," interrupted the other guard.

The Emperor's other hand shot out and hit that guard in the face.

"But you told us to say–" the guard protested.

WHACK!

"We are here to vote," the Emperor continued, "on whether the great and all conquering galaxy of Andromeda should merge with the tiny, insignificant little galaxy known as the Milky Way."

A small tentacle rose into the air somewhere near the front. The Emperor sighed. "Yes?"

"When you say 'merge'…" a small voice began hesitantly.

"I mean take over and enslave, of course."

"But–"

"Zap her!" the Emperor yelled.

"Which one?" asked a guard.

"The one over there who interrupted me of course!" the Emperor barked.

"No, I mean which guard?"

"Any!" the Emperor fumed.

"It will mean letting go of the pole."

"In the name of Andromeda, I will do it myself!" The Emperor's super springy hand shot out and looped round one of the guards' guns. There was a flash, a zap, then silence.

"Now," the Emperor continued, "any more questions? Good. In that case, let the voting commence."

From the middle of the stage rose a circle of pedestals with green and purple buttons on them. I watched as various aliens shuffled, flew or floated down to the front to vote. It was an ideal time to escape, except that I didn't want to. That thing in the hammock wanted to take over the Milky Way! I tried to get nearer the front to see how the voting was going. The pedestals were lighting up depending on what button was being pressed. The

Emperor seemed to get angrier when a pedestal lit up green so I guessed the aliens who pressed that were voting against him. Sure enough, the ones who did were then hurrying off out of the room as though running for their lives.

Soon everyone had either sat down or scarpered. There were lots of green pedestals lit up but also plenty of purple ones too. It was impossible to tell what the result of the vote was.

"The result of the vote is obvious," the Emperor bellowed. "The Milky Way will be enslaved – I mean, merged – with Andromeda with immediate effect, or at least as soon as the paperwork has been filled in. Soon the jewel of the solar system will be mine!" He pointed with his weirdly tiny hand to the view of Earth out of the window and gave a barking laugh that ended with a squelch.

One of the guards holding a pole of the hammock coughed nervously. "Er... All hail Emperor Iko Iko Iko and all that. The Solar System hasn't voted yet."

"The what?"

"The Solar System. The one we are in now. The one that includes Earth."

The Emperor burst out laughing again. It was an unpleasant sound and if I'd made it at the dinner table Mary would have sent me to my room. "None of the ape-like Earthlings in this solar system bothered to turn up. All those Asbi's we put on Earth as portals were never used. But that doesn't matter. They're all ready for their real purpose: allowing us instant access to Earth any time we want. I hereby declare that the Milky Way is henceforth ruled by Andromeda for ever and ever, no returns."

"As soon as the paperwork is filled in," added the guard.

WHACK!

"And now," announced the Emperor, "for the entertainment!"

He lifted his little hand and some tiny terrified creatures with one eye and three mouths shuffled in and started singing about how brilliant and brave and amazing the Emperor was. It was awful. The

Milky Way being taken over I mean, not the singers, although they were terrible as well. I stood there motionless with shock.

"You! Get back to work," the lizardy creature said, hitting me lightly over the head with a tray as he passed. I didn't react. I was stunned. The Milky Way had been taken over, right before my eyes, and I couldn't do a thing about it.

Or could I?

5

TURNS OUT I'M A SLIME PRINCE
- IS THAT GOOD OR BAD
OR WHAT?

"I'm here!" I yelled before I could stop myself. "I'm from the Solar System! I'll vote!"

Nobody heard me. Everyone was listening to the appalling singing, except those who were trying not to listen to it who had covered up their ears, or ear.

"I need to vote!" I shouted. I pushed my tray onto somebody's lap and ran down the steps towards the stage.

Before anyone could stop me, I dived for a pedestal. The green button was much smaller than the purple one and it took a few jabs to get the pedestal to light up, but at last it did.

"Who's that? Zap him!" the Emperor shouted.

"Too late, Your Triple Iko-ness," one of the guards said. "The Earthling has voted."

I stood there proudly. It was the bravest thing I'd ever done. And all of a sudden I realised I'd made a terrible mistake.

Because I wasn't an Earthling, was I? I was from... Triangle something? I didn't know exactly, but I did know it wasn't Earth. I had cheated. Not on purpose, but nobody here knew that. I was an imposter. I had to scarper before anyone found out.

"Well, if that's done I'll be off then," I said in a small voice. I pulled my hat down a bit more to try and cover my face. "Bye then. Byeeee."

I tiptoed to the edge of the stage. The one-eyed singers had stopped and were staring at me, open-mouthed times three. I gave them a prompt.

"Iko Iko Iko is the greatest, and his spines are wondrously long... join in, you know the words."

As the terrible singing started afresh, I galloped back up the steps. All I had to do was find the hidden door and I'd be back in Asbi's again. The lovely, normal Asbi's in lovely, normal Little Blanding. I'd dash home (lovely, normal home) and tell Mary and Bill (lovely, normal-ish Mary and Bill) all about it. They'd protect me from a giant spiny alien emperor, wouldn't they?

"Stop right there!" It was the suited lizard who'd been bossing me about all evening. He grabbed my shoulders with his strong lizardy hands. "You're not a waiter at all, are you? Why did you take that tray of flibberslurp off me if you're not a waiter?"

"Erm… because I like flibberslurp?" I offered. "Sorry, got to go." I detached his hands, which was quite difficult, and dodged past him, straight into the stomach of a big pink blob.

"Blob," the blob said, handing me my hat which had been knocked off in the collision.

I heard a gasp from somewhere. A tentacle pointed at me, then a wing. An eye on a stalk popped up in amazement.

"Look!" someone shouted. "He's got green hair!"

"It's the long-lost Slime Prince!" someone else shouted.

"Blob," the blob said.

The lizard waiter threw himself on the floor in front of me. "Slime Prince of Gloop! And I made you serve snacks like a… like a commoner! Can you ever forgive me?"

Slime Prince of what? As if sensing my confusion, a firm and comforting arm suddenly wrapped around my shoulder.

"Your Royal Greenness! Why, I can scarcely believe my senses. You're safe, after all these years!"

Before I could see who was talking, I was buried in a hug by a tall figure and a familiar smell filled my nostrils. Something I hadn't smelled for a long, long time. It was the smell of home. Not Earth. Not even Little Blanding. Somewhere else far away.

The alien who was hugging me pulled back and looked at me fondly. She wore a long cloak and was tall and thin with a green diamond on her forehead and eyebrows like pointed rooftops.

"My spaceship is nearby, Your Royal Greenness," she said in a smooth, deep voice. "Perhaps it would be wise for us to leave before you attract too much… er… attention."

We both glanced down at the stage where the Emperor was shouting out commands. The word 'zap' seemed to play a large part in them, as did the words 'cheat' and 'imposter'. Luckily the guards were struggling to try and equip their ray guns while still holding their poles and being whacked in the face.

"We can be back on Gloop in five Earth days, Your Royal Greenness."

"Where?" I asked. "And who did you say I was?"

The tall alien seemed to take that as a yes and started manoeuvring me through the crowd, which parted with some "oohs" and "aahs", and also some "parps" and "sproinks". It was just like I was famous – well, except for the parps and sproinks.

"Let's start with who I am. My name is Grek,

Slime Minister of Gloop."

"And you said I'm the Slime King?"

"Slime Prince. Your father is Slime King. This way, Your Royal Greenness."

My father? I had so many questions – even more than usual. But Grek was already pushing me towards a large silver door. It slid open to reveal a huge hangar full of spaceships of all different shapes and sizes. It was like being on the set of Cosmos Wars.

"Here is my ship – which is, of course, your ship," Grek said, leading me past various crafts to where a triangular green spaceship the length of a coach sat, lights glowing. "'The Big Green Space Busting-Machine.' Your father named it, of course."

I had a father. A dad. And he had a spaceship. Wow.

"The Royal Suite awaits," Grek said. "After you, Your Royal Greenness."

"You mean, I'm going with you? To where, again?"

"Gloop, the slime capital of the Triangulum Galaxy. Your home."

"Just like that? But my family–"

"Have been searching for you for years. Their Royal Sliminesses will be overjoyed."

"Slime again."

"It is a precious substance on Gloop, Your Royal Greenness."

"But still. Slime."

Grek took me by the arm. "Forget the slime for a moment. This is your destiny."

I pulled away. "Okay, but how about I just pop home and say goodbye to Mary and Bill and Holly? They're my family too and–"

"I am sorry, Your Royal Greenness. The vortex in the fabric of space and time that will allow us to get to Gloop closes in..." she checked a device on her little finger, "...five Earth minutes."

I took a deep breath. I had real parents, and I could meet them. I could see my real home at last. But I'd have to leave Earth and everything I'd ever known to go alone to a strange galaxy. Full of slime.

"Your Royal Greenness. I must have your answer. Are you coming or not?"

"Not without me he isn't!" yelled a voice.

I turned round to see a familiar figure in jeans and t-shirt running towards us at top speed.

"I'm his personal assistant," Holly puffed, bending over to catch her breath. "I do everything for him. He can't wipe his nose without me, can you Your Royal…"

"Greenness," I said, and grinned. "No, I can't."

"Very well. I cannot deny the Slime Prince his wish. But we must hurry. Please board the ship. Your destiny awaits you."

"But how…?" I mouthed to Holly as Grek turned her back and walked towards the ship, her cloak sweeping the ground behind her.

"Unexpected item in bagging area." Holly grinned. "You're not the only one who was curious. Come on, Your Royal Snotface. You know you can't do it without me."

And we exchanged amazed looks as we took our first steps towards the spaceship and our new future.

TURNS OUT SLIME ISN'T
THAT BAD AFTER ALL

Turns out Holly had taken a photo of Mary's invitation before she'd shown it to me, so she'd been able to scan the barcode at the Asbi's self-service checkout as well.

"Everyone was looking for you," Holly told me as we climbed up a ramp into the belly of the ship, "and so was I until I realised you'd probably followed the instructions on the letter. That's when I sneaked off to do the same. When I got here a giant raisin stuffed some sort of headphone thing on me and suddenly I could hear loads of aliens saying the Slime Prince had returned. It took me a while to work out they meant my dorky little foster brother.

Oh, and guess who I saw?"

"I know. The alien with one leg coming out of the top of its head. Brilliant."

"No, it was–"

"The one that looked like a giant big toe."

"No, it was–"

"The one with the seven butts? That's a Parpoid, that is. I learned that when I was being an alien waiter."

Holly groaned with exasperation. "No! It was Harry Handsome."

"Harry Horriblesome? You see him everywhere!"

"This way, Your Royal Greenness," Grek interrupted, grandly waving a hand towards an impressively large suite of rooms. "And there is a small room next door for your servant. Well, it's currently a broom cupboard but we can clear it out."

"Hey," protested Holly, but that was all I heard as Grek swept me into the luxurious rooms and closed the door. I instantly forgot about Holly as I gazed around me in awe. The main room was dotted with futuristic-looking couches, chairs and little tables. In the middle of the floor was a huge sunken bath thing. But the main feature was the view. Floor-to-ceiling windows lined one side and I could already see a small white sphere moving slowly away from us, leaving a vast blackness studded with stars.

"We're moving already!"

"The Big Green Space-Busting Machine is a very smooth ride, Your Greenness."

I ran to the windows. "Hang on, were we just on the moon?"

"It offered the best view of Earth. The Emperor was very particular about that. He wanted to look at his prize."

I craned to see Earth but it was too late. I felt a surge of homesickness mixed with guilt and topped with a layer of fear, all served on a bed of anxiety.

"He's going to take over the Milky Way, isn't he?" I said, imagining Mary and Bill in chains being shouted at by a three-eyed monster.

"Your Greenness, this is none of your concern. You have much more important things to think about. Such as: what would you like for your lunch?"

Suddenly I realised I was starving. All I'd eaten since lunch were some chocolate teaspoons. Mary and Bill instantly disappeared from my head as Grek began to explain all about Triangulum food and took me through the menu options.

★★★

There were two brilliant things about the spaceship. One – it was a spaceship. Whoop whoop! And two – I was treated like a prince. A Slime Prince, yes, but still a prince. My rooms were called the Slime Suite, and the great big sunken bath in the middle was filled with fresh slime every day.

Holly had that job. It was probably her least favourite thing she had to do, after bringing me my meals. I don't know why she complained all the time. She was allowed to finish anything I didn't, so she got to eat almost as well as I did. I always made sure I left her something. And I let her look out of the windows. But she had to leave when Grek was there. Grek liked our little talks to be private, which was fair enough. Holly had plenty to do in the kitchen making my next meal anyway.

Grek came every day to tell me about my home planet, Gloop. She explained that plenty of people wanted to get their hands on Gloop's precious slime, so there were lots of wars there, and it was during the last one that I was kidnapped.

"By the Andromedans," I said, hoping to impress Grek with the one thing I knew about myself.

"That is correct, Your Royal Greenness. Emperor Iko Iko Iko was hoping your parents would hand over control of Gloop to save you. They didn't, but he took it anyway."

Grek showed me a mug with a triangular handle. On it was a picture of two people wearing crowns and holding a baby. The baby had a tuft of green hair.

"That's me!" I grabbed the mug and stared at myself. I looked surprised. On the mug, I mean, but probably in real life too. "So these are…" I gulped, "my parents?"

"This is a commemorative mug celebrating your birthday," Grek explained. "Every citizen of Gloop was given one. This is your father and mother, the Slime King and Queen of Gloop."

My dad looked like a big version of me: short-ish and happy-looking with a round face. My mum was also smiling, but she seemed a bit anxious, almost like she knew someone could come and nick me at any time. And she'd been right.

"So why didn't they?" I asked.

"Why didn't they what, Your Royal Greenness?"

"Hand over Gloop to save me." Okay, my kidnappers had demanded a whole galaxy, but surely if my parents had really loved me they would have given anything to save me?

"A rescue plan was in place," Grek said.

"I myself was involved. But something happened that made all our plans useless. For the first time ever, a prisoner escaped from the Andromeda Mega Jail. And took you with them."

"Bill!" I muttered.

"What?" Grek said.

I paused. "Nothing." For some reason I didn't want to involve Bill. Maybe it was because thinking about him and Mary might make me have second thoughts, and it was too late for that.

"Why don't you keep it, Your Greenness?" Grek said, nodding at the mug.

My parents smiled up at me.

"Are you sure? I mean, it's yours."

"It's only a mug." Grek stood up. "I will have your servant bring in refreshments. Have you tried the slime bath yet?"

"Er, no."

Every day Grek kept on at me to get in the slime.

"You might enjoy it. We only have a few days before we reach Gloop. You should be familiar with your heritage." She arched her pointy eyebrows even further as the door slid closed behind her.

I bent down and touched the slime in the bath. It was cold and green, like I imagined a gooseberry jelly would be if I'd ever touched one of those. Still, it was my heritage. Maybe I should give it a go. I'd done worse things, like used the school showers. I whipped off my clothes and slid in. Imagine sliding into gooseberry jelly. It's not as bad as it sounds. I leaned back and closed my eyes.

"What are you doing?" Holly snorted, entering with a loaded tray.

I quickly burrowed down in slime up to the neck. "It's my heritage."

"It's disgusting, that's what it is. Here, I've brought Your Weirdness some snacks, as ordered." She bent down and prodded a finger at the slime. "Yeuch!"

"It's not that bad when you get used to it. Look, it holds you up."

"No, you stay down there. I'll take your word for

it." Holly sat cross-legged on the floor next to me and bit into a twisty multi-coloured bar. She chucked one to me and we munched for a while, staring out of the windows. Stars twinkled, and in the distance a beautiful spiral shimmered.

"Grek says that's the Triangulum Galaxy," I said. "Where I was born."

Holly wiped her mouth with the back of her hand. "I know. The servants were talking about it. They think I'm one of them, it's really annoying."

"Why don't you just say you're my foster sister?"

Holly looked embarrassed. "I thought if I pretended I was your assistant, they'd be more likely to let me come and… you know. Keep an eye on you. Obviously I'm regretting that now."

"Saying you're my assistant or coming to keep an eye on me?"

Holly finished her mouthful and gestured at the window. "What do you think, slime-for-brains? We're in space, aren't we? This is once-in-a-lifetime stuff."

"But what if we don't get to go back? What if we never see Mary and Bill ever again?" My voice cracked and I stared hard at a strangely shaped rock as it drifted past the window.

"Mary and Bill are liars. We can't trust them anymore. Do you want foster parents you can't trust?"

The rock slid slowly out of sight.

"They're not liars, they're space explorers who didn't tell us," I said firmly. And that reminded me. I had been thinking of Mary and Bill as they always had been: nice and dull. I'd forgotten their secret pasts getting stuck in the cleft of Twin Cheeks and dancing with Centauri Ambassadors. "I bet when they realise what's happened, they'll come and join us."

Holly didn't look convinced. "Whatever." She dipped her fingers in the bath and flicked a piece of slime at me. "Now get out of that swamp and come and explore the ship with me. I've found some amazing stuff while you've been shut up in here doing history of Gloop lessons."

After that conversation with Holly, I actually felt a lot better. Maybe Mary and Bill weren't sitting at home worrying about us after all. Maybe they had found out and were charging up their ray guns and turbo boosting their secret spaceships. Or maybe they were just happy for me to discover my true identity.

Either way, there was loads on the ship to keep my mind off Earth. Like the zero-G room where you could bounce off the walls and ceiling just for fun. Or the cockpit where the pilot told me never to enter again if I wanted to get to Triangulum in one piece because I didn't stop asking her questions. Or the games room where you moved big, yellow squares across a wall for no reason at all. Grek said I was a natural, but I think she was just being polite.

The meals were interesting too, especially when

Grek explained what they were and how to eat them. She even put a little bit of slime on my plate each day, saying it was a delicacy fit for royal blood. Holly wasn't allowed to have any. She claimed she was pleased but I bet she was jealous really. At least she had the honour of dishing it up for me, although when I explained that to her, I ended up with some in my face.

On the fifth day, Grek came in to wake me up.

"Are we nearly there yet?" I asked, as I had always done on every car journey since the beginning of time.

Grek swept her arm out towards the window. She loved a big gesture. "Your home planet of Gloop is just a few hours away. For this special occasion, you will take a slime bath and then your servant will dress you." She clicked her fingers and Holly stomped in with a pile of clothing draped over her arm which she dumped on the floor.

"I'm bringing his clothes but I'm not dressing him," she said in disgust. "Dress yourself, your

Mouldiness."

As Holly flounced out, Grek raised a critical eyebrow. "When we reach Gloop I will ensure you have the best servants in Triangulum, Your Royal Greenness."

"Oh, that's okay," I said quickly. "It's just her way."

"But she doesn't even wear a uniform, just the face of a slightly confused but aesthetically pleasing human being on her torso."

"That's Harry Handsome. You must have heard of Harry Handsome?"

Grek shook her head. She was lucky. I wished I'd never heard of him.

Grek gave me my clothes to put on. They were a bit weird. I mean, I'd expected something royal like a red cloak and maybe even a sword and a crown.

"It's a green boiler suit," I said, holding it up.

"Of course, Your Royal Greenness. Nobody else on Gloop is allowed to wear green apart from you."

"And is anyone else allowed to wear a boiler

suit?"

"Of course not."

That sounded a bit better. "What about my crown?"

"You will be crowned prince in a magnificent welcome ceremony after you arrive on Gloop. And now I will leave you to prepare yourself." Grek paused at the door. "Don't forget the slime bath, Your Royal Greenness."

Grek was certainly very keen on me spending time in the slime. But I wasn't arguing. Believe it or not, I was actually starting to enjoy it. I wallowed in green ooze for a while, then put on my princely attire.

A green boiler suit. It was a bit of a let-down, to be honest. I even had to wear my jeans underneath. But at least I didn't have to wear a hat. No need to be ashamed of anything green on Gloop.

"You look like a frog," Holly said when she came back in. "I mean, even more of a frog."

"Ha ha. Can you believe Grek doesn't know who

Harry Handsome is?" I said.

Holly looked thoughtful. "Don't you think it's weird that I saw him?"

"Not really. You're always seeing him. You said you saw him in Asbi's last week, and it turned out to be a floor mop."

"I thought it was him from the back."

"You were nearly right. It was just like him but with a personality."

"Very funny, Frog Features. So you think I just imagined it?"

"Maybe. Or maybe there are so many different sorts of aliens that, by the law of averages, there has to be one that looks exactly like Harry Handsome."

Holly shook her head firmly. "Never. There's only one Harry Handsome."

"Well that's good news anyway," I said, backing away from Holly in anticipation.

"I really will push you into that slime bath in a minute, Your Royal Bogeyface."

TURNS OUT SOMEONE'S BEEN TELLING FIBS

Our arrival on Gloop, the slime capital of the Triangulum Galaxy, was amazing. The spaceship docked on a giant pedestal in the middle of a square surrounded by tall, silver buildings. I got to walk down the steps on a green carpet. Crowds of short people with round faces and greenish skin waved green flags and cheered. I felt right at home.

The only slightly weird thing was that, before we got out, Grek jammed a miner's helmet, complete with lamp, on my head.

"Solidarity," she'd said.

"What?"

"The slimers – slime miners – will love it."

They certainly did. Everyone was going mad. I wondered if this was what it must feel like to be Harry Handsome.

"Do you think I should make a speech?" I asked Holly. I still had the GarbleGadget in, so I knew the crowd would be able to understand me. "How about 'Hello Gloop, it's good to be back?'"

"You're the prince," Holly said, but before I could clear my throat Grek appeared in front of me, elbowing Holly aside.

"I expect you are tired after your long trip," she said. "Come with me and I will find a place for you to rest."

"I just have rested. For five days," I pointed out. "And I'm just about to make a brilliant speech. Can I take the miner's helmet off now?"

Grek ignored me. "Space travel is so taxing, especially for those of royal blood who are that bit more delicate than the rest of us."

Before I could protest further, Grek was already hustling me off towards a silver hemisphere the size of a small car.

"Hang on, where's Holly?" I asked as she bundled me in.

"Oh don't worry, she'll be right behind us," Grek said, settling herself on a soft chair.

Reluctantly, I sat opposite her. As soon as my bottom hit the chair, a metal seat belt sprung across my lap and closed with a firm clunk. Then two more people got in, one each side, sandwiching me in like a piece of ham. They were dressed in black uniforms and had long sticks with glowing ends tucked into their belts.

"We wouldn't want you to be kidnapped again, would we?" Grek said, detaching a remote control from the wall and choosing a button.

"Are we going to meet my parents now?" I asked, trying to peer around the guards.

"Yes, that's right," Grek said, smiling widely. "Off to the royal palace we go."

We zoomed smoothly off down a wide street lined with bubble-shaped houses. I eagerly looked out for some sort of big palace, but the houses soon disappeared and we were whizzing across a barren landscape of sludgy green and black.

"We're definitely going to the palace to see my parents?"

"That's right." Grek's eyes slid towards the button she had just pressed on the remote. It had been the yellow one. I narrowed my eyes. The GarbleGadget must have done something to my brain as well, as I just could about read it.

Slime mines.

Uh-oh. Suddenly things were slotting into place, and the places they were slotting into were not the places I wanted them to slot into, if you see what I mean.

"Hang on. Something's not right."

"And what might that be?" Grek asked, arching her eyebrows.

"You're not calling me Your Royal Greenness anymore, like you normally insist on doing every other sentence. And we're not going to the palace.

We're going to the slime mines. Aren't we?"

Grek's eyes went cold.

"It would be easier if you didn't struggle."

My hunch was right. Suddenly everything flipped around in my head. Grek wasn't helping me. She was kidnapping me! But what could I do? Struggle, yes. That was a good idea. I tried, but the two guards gripped my arms.

Grek sighed, as though me finding out her evil plans was just mildly annoying. "I may have told a few teensy weensy lies, but it's for the good of the planet. While there's no heir to the throne, it's so much easier for someone to step in and take control."

"You, you mean."

Grek just smiled smugly.

"But the crowds! Won't they wonder why I'm not there? They were cheering."

"Cheering for me. On pain of death. They don't know you're here and never will."

"And my parents?" I asked, heart sinking.

"Ditto."

"You're Andromedan!" I gasped as the final penny slotted into the final slot with an unwelcome plop. No wonder Grek had been so happy to give away her royal commemorative mug.

Grek sat back in her chair, as though flattered to be asked about her heritage. "Not Andromedan by birth. But as soon as I reached maturity I applied for citizenship. I had to keep it a secret, of course. Andromeda is not popular. I have no idea why. It is superior to every galaxy in every way, as any Andromedan will tell you."

"Well, there's the first clue," I muttered.

"All the other planets in this pesky little galaxy have given in and accepted their new rulers," Grek continued. "All except Gloop."

I struggled again but my captors held me firm. "What about Earth? And all of the Milky Way? They'll never accept being part of Andromeda, you wait and see."

"They'll have no choice, not after your illegal

vote." Grek smiled. "Andromeda will certainly be taking over the Creamy Way, just as soon as the paperwork is sorted out."

"It's the Milky Way!" I yelled. "And I grew up on Earth – doesn't that make my vote count?"

Grek sighed theatrically. "I'd love to discuss the complexities of the Local Group voting system with you, but I'm afraid we've run out of time. Welcome to the slime mines, *Your Royal Greenness*."

The vehicle had come to a stop. The two guards dragged me out after Grek but kept hold of me. We were in a large, busy area filled with chains of people passing buckets of slime to each other which were eventually tipped into even bigger buckets. These were tipped into even bigger buckets until the buckets were buckets on wheels and got driven away. It didn't seem to be a very good system and lots of slime was getting slopped onto the ground which made it slippery.

"They're all wearing green boiler suits just like mine!" I exclaimed.

"Oh yes. Another teensy weensy lie. But you did want to fit in, didn't you?" Grek said, striding ahead and knocking people out of her way.

"Help me!" I shouted to a boiler-suited man. His face stayed blank as he passed his bucket to the next person in the line.

"There's no point talking to the slimers," Grek said over her shoulder. "For some reason, terrible conditions and no pay has sapped the life out of them. Miserable creatures."

We went down a slope into a large entrance. The walls were lit with dull, green lights and I realised we were underground. More slimers trudged past with buckets, taking no notice of us.

"BING BONG! KEEP WORKING. BING BONG! A SLIMEY MINER IS A HAPPY MINER."

"What was that?" I asked Grek.

"Just some encouraging messages for the slimers."

"BING BONG! IT'S GOOD TO WORK FOR

FREE," said the rich, deep voice, like honey sliding off a spoon.

"Is that your voice, Grek? It sounds like your voice. Is it?"

Grek turned around again and stopped, causing the guards holding me to crash into her.

"Do you have to ask so many questions all the time?"

"It is though, isn't it?"

Grek didn't answer but pushed me into a side room. Hooks with boiler suits and helmets on them lined the wall. Grek took a helmet for herself and chucked a couple to her henchmen.

"Why are we here?" I asked.

Grek glared at me. "From now on, you can figure out the answers."

I would have been scared at this point but Grek's helmet was too small and she looked ridiculous, like she had an extra tiny head on top of her real one.

We passed into a featureless tunnel. The lights from the guards' and Grek's helmets lit the way.

Slimers scraped the walls with their hands, the lights on their own helmets showing green seams in the rock face. Buckets beneath collected the ooze. The floor was slippery and we had to slow down to avoid falling over. Suddenly I was glad I was wearing a helmet after all.

"Before you ask, yes we could do it all by machine, but it gives the wretched creatures something to do besides resisting oppression," Grek commented.

We ducked under some warning signs and into a smaller, narrower tunnel. Grek broke through some tape that looked a bit like the sort of thing used to block off a crime scene.

"Erm, should we be going down here? What about health and safety? I think I'll go back now, if it's all the same to you," I said, trying to twist away from my captors. "See you later."

The guard holding me tightened his grip and gave me an extra shove.

"Nice try," Grek said, from somewhere ahead.

It was getting harder to see down this new tunnel. The lamps on our helmets were the only source of light now. Grek kicked away some rotten boards.

"Here we are. Well, Your Royal Greenness, it's been interesting meeting you again. Do you know, I held you when you were a baby? Quite frankly it was revolting. All that cooing and dribbling. And you haven't changed much since."

"You have. You're even uglier."

"Very good. But Andromedans don't value beauty. They value power. Luckily I have plenty of that – or I will have when your family is completely extinguished."

"You're a liar!" I said, struggling against the guard's grip.

"I prefer to use the term 'factually challenged'. And I didn't lie about everything. I told you you were going to meet your parents, and you are."

Grek stepped aside and gestured to the guard holding me, who released my arm and pushed me through the broken boards into a dark space. One of my feet slipped sending a stone clattering down below and I realised I was on the edge of a large hole filled with blackness.

"An abandoned mineshaft," Grek explained cheerfully. "Enjoy the experience. It will be the last one you ever have."

"Just one more question," I said. "You owe me that, at least."

As I had hoped, Grek loved the sound of her own voice. "Very well. Just one more."

"The thing I wanted to ask you…" I began, slowly sidling around the hole, "…what I really want to know is why you, Grek, the Slime Minister of Gloop, the place we are in now, are such a complete and utter… berk."

The long sentence had allowed me to move back to Grek and the guards again. I ducked under the last guard's arm and made a run for it. The narrow tunnel stretched out before me, but I was a good sprinter. I'd run away from Holly when she'd chased me out of her bedroom millions of times.

I got to the end and turned the corner into the main tunnel where the slimers were working. Everything would have been perfect if the ground hadn't been covered in slime. Before I knew it I was on my back, my helmet skidding off down the tunnel, and the guards were standing over me, their lights blaring into my eyes.

"You were rubbish at running when you were a baby, as well," Grek commented unnecessarily. "Pick him up and this time don't let him go!"

"Help!" I pleaded again, but the slimers only looked at me helplessly. I guessed they had seen this sort of thing before. I was dragged away from them and back down the narrow tunnel towards the hole. The guards tried to push me in. I had a good old kick at their legs as we all teetered round the hole like we were performing a really rubbish dance.

"Hey!" protested a guard as I stamped on his toe, revealing that he had learned to speak at some point in his life after all. He bent to grab his toe, and I swiped his helmet and hit the other guard with it, who dropped to the ground with a groan.

"Oh for Andromeda's sake," Grek complained, and she walked forward and gave me a short, sharp prod.

I stumbled backwards towards the hole, trod into empty space and felt myself falling. At least I had the helmet for health and safety. I landed on my feet for one miraculous moment, then tumbled over and ended up on my back. Above me was a small hole where two beams of light shone down.

"It's quite nice in here actually," I said in a loud, carefree voice, trying to ignore all the bits of my body which were complaining like mad. "You shouldn't have gone to all this trouble."

"You were rubbish at sarcasm as a baby too," Grek said, her voice echoing into the chamber.

The lights moved away. Then I heard a clunk. It sounded like some sort of cover had been put over the hole. I braced myself for a volley of evil laughter, but it didn't come. Perhaps Grek was saving it for higher up where the acoustics were better.

Groaning, I reached for the helmet and its friendly lamp and put it on my head. The bits I could see were just bare rock with a few veins of slime. Tunnel openings led off at intervals all around me. But I didn't hold out any hope. Grek had said this was an abandoned section. They would all be dead ends.

I stood there in the almost-dark, staring at a spotlighted patch of slime. I had come so far, to a distant galaxy I'd never heard of, ready to meet my parents and find out, finally, who I was. I had given up everything. For what? A blob of slime on a wall.

I thought of Mary and Bill. Had they guessed where I'd gone yet? Could they even do anything about it? Then I remembered. Earth was going to be taken over by Andromeda. Mary and Bill would have much bigger things to worry about. Who knew what would happen with Emperor Spineypants in charge?

And where was Holly? Was she a prisoner too?

Maybe she had made it to the palace. Maybe she had found my parents and they were already looking for me. But Grek had said I was still going to meet them. What had she meant by that?

I shivered as all sorts of scary thoughts crowded into my mind, most of them involving piles of bones and ghosts. I closed my eyes but that just made things worse. I would have to explore, and make sure there were no bones and no ghosts. Maybe there would even be a way out. If not, time would pass and eventually I would be the bones and the ghost. I shivered again, and picked a tunnel.

8

TURNS OUT I DO HAVE PARENTS - WELL, SORT OF

I don't know how long I was wandering those tunnels. My watch had smashed in the fall so I could only measure time by my stomach rumbling. Eventually it rumbled so much I figured I had missed at least three meals and I tried licking a wall. The now familiar taste of slime filled my mouth and soon I was scraping it off like a proper slimer.

All the tunnels I had found so far were dead ends, just finishing in rock. I hadn't even found any bones. There was nothing but rock, soil, slime, rock and more slime.

So you can imagine how excited I was when I heard a voice.

At first I couldn't make out the words, just human-sounding noises. I turned my head and my helmet light flashed around the tunnel. I was in the fifth tunnel from the left by then, which was my least favourite tunnel so far. Not because it was worse than any of the other tunnels. It was just that the novelty of wandering along dark corridors with nothing in them was wearing off big time.

There was no one there. Nothing but the same rock and slime.

Great. Just to add to my troubles, I was now hearing voices in my head. Apparently being in solitary confinement for long periods could drive you mad. It had just happened a bit quickly to me, that was all.

Or... the voices were coming from one of the other tunnels, and were just carrying very clearly. Maybe the acoustics *were* good down here. Grek should have stayed and done her evil laugh here after all. Assuming a crouching position, I crept out of Five and into Tunnel Number Six.

"I promise you, you didn't leave the gas on," a patient-sounding voice said.

"But what if I did?" The other voice was higher and more worried.

"It's been ten years. If you'd left it on, we'd know by now."

"But we're too far away to hear the explosion!"

The first voice sighed. I crept forward. There was a bend ahead. The two people speaking had to be just round the corner. I turned my helmet light off and inched nearer, keeping one hand on the wall for guidance.

"What if I forgot to unplug the toaster?"

"It doesn't matter." The patient voice was sounding rather less patient now.

"But it heats up. Doesn't it? The plug I mean. It'll heat up and explode. And what if we left bread in it? There'll be crumbs everywhere!"

I turned the corner. It was pitch black. Were these people talking in the dark? I would have to put my light on, and then they would know I was there. But

I couldn't risk stumbling into them. They might not take kindly to that either. I took a deep breath and turned on the helmet light.

Nothing. There was nobody there, down the whole tunnel, which I could just about see finished in another dead end.

I smiled to myself. Now that it had happened, going mad was actually a relief. I wouldn't be alone anymore because there would be imaginary people in my head to talk to. I skipped to the end of the tunnel, just for fun, and started singing a song I remembered from Cubs called Alice the Camel.

"There's somebody in here!" the higher voice said, sounding shocked.

"It's me! Alice the camel!" I yelled. "Alice the camel has three humps, so go Alice go, boom boom boom!"

"Whoever they are, they're unhinged," the other voice said.

This was brilliant! The imaginary voices were already talking back to me. They would be great company for the days ahead until I finally withered up and died.

"Alice the camel has no humps, coz Alice was a horse!" I sung.

"How odd. I recognise that," the high voice said.

"Do you, dear? I've never even heard of Alice the camel."

"No, that voice. Of course, it was only saying goo-goo-ga-ga when I last heard it, but I do recognise the pitch and tone. Don't you?"

I had stopped singing. The voices were sounding a bit too logical to be imaginary. Not *very* logical, mind you, but a bit. Maybe I just couldn't see them? Maybe they really were here after all, but in yet another tunnel? I rushed off back to the main chamber.

"Wait! Don't goooooo!" cried a voice, trailing off.

There were people here and I was going to find them. I set off down Tunnel Number Six. I also tried Seven, Eight, Nine and Ten. In Eight, I found a crack at the bottom of the wall that I could stick my hand through, but it didn't help me. Ten was my new least favourite. It didn't even have a bend to make it interesting.

I collapsed in an exhausted heap and dreamed about wandering round a maze of dark corridors. Then I got up and carried on. It was hard to tell sleeping from waking, to be honest.

Eventually I got confused about which tunnel I'd heard the voices in originally. My new plan was to head back there, but all the tunnels spiralled off the main chamber and I wasn't sure which one I'd started in. After a brief meal of slime, which was tasting better every time only because I was so hungry, I randomly staggered into the nearest tunnel and suddenly I could hear them again.

"I wish he'd come back," said the worried voice. "Do you think it really was him?"

"Yes," said the lower voice. "But we must try not to get our hopes up. Grek could have thrown anyone in here. We won't know unless we see him properly."

They sounded trustworthy. They sounded nice. "I'm here," I said tiredly.

I heard some excited mutterings.

"We're coming towards you. We should be there in about half an hour."

"Half an hour!" I repeated. "Where are you?"

"Just over there by your feet. To the left, next to the wall."

I took a step forward.

"Look out!" the voices shrieked.

I crouched down and trained my light on the floor. Just a few inches from my foot were two slugs. And that was also where the voices were coming from.

"Turn the light on yourself so we can see you," the lower voice said.

Talking slugs, and bossy ones too. I took off the helmet and crouched down, turning the light towards my face and making myself flinch with the sudden brightness.

"It is him!" squeaked the higher voice. There was a sigh followed by a plop.

"She's fainted," the other slug said. "Quick, put the helmet on the ground so we can all see."

I did as I was told – the slug had a very commanding voice. The light from the helmet made a small bright pool and I could see the bigger slug leaning over the other one which was lying motionless on its side.

What were you supposed to do if someone fainted? "You need to put her in the recovery position," I suggested. "One leg over the other, and one arm… oh. Sorry." The only arms and legs around here were mine.

"It's all right, she's coming round."

The smaller slug stirred and looked up at me. I say looked, but I couldn't see her eyes, just two antennae stretching towards me.

"My son. It really is you. He hasn't changed a bit, has he, darling?" she added.

"Apart from being ten years older and a walking,

talking giant I suppose not," the big slug said, his antennae waggling in my direction. "You don't recognise our voices, do you?"

They seemed nice, for slugs, so I tried to put aside what they had said about being my parents and go with the flow.

"Erm, no," I said, kneeling down.

"Let me try," the small slug said, and moving into a more upright position she began to sing:

"Hush little green one, don't you peep,
Mummy's got a slime song to send you to sleep.
If that slime doesn't make you snore,
Mummy's got some more slime that she can pour.
If that slime doesn't make you snooze,
Mummy's got some more slime that she can ooze.
If that slime—"

"Wait a minute!" I said. My eyelids were drooping and I snapped them back open. Something was stirring inside. I thought back to what I'd always believed was my earliest memory – my mother screaming and my father telling the nurse to take me away. "Did anyone scream when I was born?" I asked.

"Oh no, it was a very easy birth," the small slug said.

This was all becoming very odd – and that was saying something considering what I had seen over the last few days.

"Not even when you saw I had green hair?"

"Green hair is a sign of great things," the big slug said. "It runs through the Gloop royal family, but only shows up once in every ten generations. We were thrilled."

"I remember it all so clearly," the small slug said, her antennae pointing upwards. "There were parties all over the planet and dancing in the street. We needed a strong ruler, you see. Andromeda was getting closer every day and we knew they wanted to merge. A Green Prince gave hope to all."

Wow. I had had a nice birth after all, and made people happy.

By people I meant slugs, of course. Oh, what was

I thinking? How could my parents be slugs?

The big slug took over. "All was well until your first birthday. Grek, our most trusted Slime Minister, bought you a royal spaceship. I called it the Big Green Space-Busting Machine. Good name, eh? Anyway, it was to be kept for when you came of age and travelled the galaxy for your year out. We popped you in the pilot's seat to take a photo and it shot away into space. We never saw you again."

He stopped talking and the two slugs leaned towards each other for mutual comfort. I found myself starting to believe them. Slightly.

"So why didn't you go after me?" I asked after a moment.

"We did, of course. We sent our entire space fleet after you. We waged war against Andromeda for the next six months. They won, and Gloop became part of Andromeda, just like the rest of Triangulum. We lost everything, but worst of all we lost our son."

"Grek revealed she had been working for the Andromedans all along," the small slug said, her voice shaky with emotion. "She kept us on as figureheads, but it was awful. She made everyone work in the slime mines in terrible conditions just to make her and the Emperor lots of money. We visited the mines as much as we could, to help the workers. Grek got fed up with us and threw us into this cell. We've lived here on slime ever since. We haven't been able to see each other until now." She turned to the bigger slug. "Do I look dreadful, darling?"

He bowed his head and their antennae touched. "You are as beautiful as the day I married you. Well not exactly, because you're a slug now. But I'm a slug too. And you look pretty good to me."

"Oh darling!"

I looked down at them, these two slugs who claimed to be my nearest relations, and made a decision. Feeling more positive than I had since landing on Gloop, I jumped to my feet.

"Eek!" the slugs shrieked, squirming out of the way just in time.

"Sorry. But I've got good news. I'm going to

rescue you."

"But why would you do that?"

"Because you're my parents." I was convinced. My eyes watered as I looked at them fondly. I wished I could hug them, but I'd probably squash them flat. "Mum. Dad. I'm going to take you back to the palace where you belong."

There was a pause as the big slug – or Dad as I now had to think of him – dipped his antennae. "That's very kind of you, son, but we're quite happy where we are."

"What? Here?"

"We're slugs now," Mum said. (I had a mum!) "We don't need thrones and palaces."

"And we like the slime," Dad added. "We're actually pretty happy away from all the stresses and strains of rulership. And now we know you're alive, we're *really* happy."

I crouched back down. It seemed a bit rude to be towering over my parents like a giant. "But don't you want to take back your kingdom?"

"Andromeda is a mighty galaxy," Dad said sadly. "We battled them as bravely as we could with all the resources we had, but they defeated us. There's nothing we can do about it now. You can escape, though. You can make a difference."

"But do it really carefully or I'll worry," Mum said. "And make sure you wear a vest – it can get really draughty in that palace."

This was great. I had a mum, a real one who nagged me to wear a vest! I savoured the moment.

"And check if I turned the gas off. And the toaster."

The novelty of being nagged was wearing off. Time to break the bad news.

"Mum, Dad. I can't escape. I found a tiny hole and you two can get through. But I can't. Please, save yourselves."

"What hole?" Dad asked. "Lead the way, let's have a look."

I marched off before realising that my parents hadn't moved. Or maybe they had, but not far enough for me to notice. I ran back and put my palm flat on the floor. "I can carry you there. If you don't mind."

"My big strong son," Mum said proudly as she and Dad oozed onto my hand. They were both so light I could hardly feel them.

It took me ages to find the crack again. Mum and Dad must have got a bit fed up but they didn't show it, just kept saying how proud they were being ferried about by their athletic son. I was relieved when I saw the gap in the bottom of the wall again (Tunnel Eight, for future reference). This time it was lit up, and I could hear voices from the other side. Tired, weary voices. Slimers!

"This hole must lead to the canteen," Mum explained as she and Dad peered through. Apparently they had never been this far. "Grek stopped food being served in the mine years ago but everyone still goes there on their five minute lunch break, just to smell the faint whiff of graffle chips as they lick the walls."

Dad looked up at me. "Well done, son. You can get out through here. I'll miss you, but not as much as I did before you turned up. Now off you go, before you set your mother off."

I looked at the hole, then back at my parents. They had been slugs for too long. It had altered their perception of size. "I'm not going to fit through there," I pointed out.

"Of course you are. You've just got to try."

Mum nudged him. "Don't forget, he hasn't ingested slime like we have. He may not have the power."

"Of course he has the power! He's got green hair, hasn't he?"

Power? What power? This was exciting news. "Wait – let me guess. I can walk through walls, can't I? No, I'm a shape shifter. I know – I can turn small!"

"You've sort of guessed right," Dad said. "You will be small. You just won't be…"

"Human?"

"That's right."

I let the news sink in. "My superpower is that I can turn into a slug, isn't it?"

"Technically it's less of a superpower, more of an allergy. Having royal blood makes you particularly sensitive. All you have to do is eat slime for a few more days and you'll be out of here."

I thought back to the journey in the spaceship. "But that's easy! I've been eating slime already. Grek's even had me bathing in it."

Mum didn't seem surprised. "She thinks being a slug is a terrible punishment. But it's not. You'll love it. You never know, you might even decide to stay a slug one day, just like we did."

"I don't think that's going to happen," I said with a disbelieving laugh.

Dad glanced at Mum with a flicker of worry which he quickly hid. Wow, I was learning to read the body language of slugs really well already. "Once you're into the canteen, work your way into the nearest active tunnel. Get yourself into someone's bucket of slime while they're not looking and you'll be carried back up to the surface."

"I wish you would come with me," I said.

"We're slugs now, son, and that's how we want to stay. We're happy with our lives in here, and at least we're near the slimers. We'll stay here and cover for you. Now, let's do this thing."

I listened carefully while Dad explained how to change into a slug. I'd tell you too but it wouldn't do you any good – you haven't got royal blood and green hair. Anyway, when Dad had finished he made me repeat it all back to him, and then he told me the whole thing again because I'd got some of it wrong, and after a few goes at repeating it I got it right. Well, the important parts anyway.

"Sounds easy enough," I said, trying to convince myself. "So how long do I stay a slug? When do I turn back?"

Mum and Dad exchanged worried glances again.

"You tell him," Mum said.

"You might not turn back, son," Dad said. "You

probably will, but there's a small chance you might not."

"How small a chance?"

"Seventy-five percent."

"That's not small!"

"It's smaller than eighty percent."

I groaned. I didn't want to be a slug, even if my parents did seem to love it. It just wasn't something I'd ever dreamed of, like being a pirate or a racing driver.

"You'll be alright," Mum said reassuringly. "The green hair will help."

"How?"

"I don't know, but it must do somehow. Goodbye, my precious son. It's been lovely getting to know you. And make sure you brush your teeth, that's very important."

"Yes, Mum," I said, feeling choked.

"You just get yourself somewhere safe," Dad said. "And remember, whatever happens, we're proud of you."

I reached down and gently touched their heads. Then, without saying anything because I couldn't find the words, I did what Dad had told me and turned myself into a slug.

The world seemed to expand and then suddenly, right in front of me, were two terrifying, blobby monsters. Then I realised it was Mum and Dad. We were all the same size together. Now it really did seem possible that they were my parents. They leaned in to me in a squelchy hug and for a moment I felt what it was like to have a family. A bit like when Mary and Bill hugged me, but with less arms and more antennae.

I turned away and oozed off into the crack in the wall, which was now a spacious tunnel. Very spacious. It took me ages just to get to it. I squirted out a trail and that made it quicker to move. I slid along the tunnel floor, marvelling at my long smooth body and the way my eyes seemed to float above me. This would be something to tell Holly about when we found each other. I hoped she was okay like me.

I oozed along until the tunnel became lighter. In front of me was a massive room carved out of the rock, with lots of chair and table legs. Gigantic creatures in big boots were sitting about, their huge feet promising death to any slug who wandered near. It was the canteen. I had made it.

I squirmed out of the hole. Immediately a massive shadow turned everything black and I shrank towards the wall as a huge boot came crashing down next to me.

That had been close. I had to change back before I turned into something even worse than a slug – a rubbery splat on the floor. It was only then that I realised Dad hadn't taken me through the process to turn human again. Was it because of the seventy-five percent chance that it couldn't happen? Well, I was going to try. Surely all I had to do was repeat the sequence backwards. It had to work.

Staying close to the wall to give myself the best chance of remaining unsquashed, I concentrated hard. Pretty soon everything around me began to shrink. No, I was getting bigger. The room wasn't vast and full of monsters with big feet any more. It was a normal size with normal people in it. Well, fairly normal apart from the fact that they were licking the walls. I looked down at myself. I was human too! And I had clothes on again, which was a detail I hadn't thought to worry about but which I was now very glad to see. I was even wearing the helmet again. It had worked!

"Where did you suddenly come from?" One of the slimers had broken off licking the walls and was pointing at me.

I took a deep breath. This was going to be an important moment, for me and for my subjects. When they saw my green hair they would fall to the ground in awe, just like the aliens had at the meeting. (Well, a few of them. Well, one.) I paused for dramatic effect, then slowly reached up to remove my helmet.

"BING BONG!" chimed a loudspeaker. Grek's

voice filled the room. "LUNCH TIME HAS FINISHED. RETURN TO YOUR SLIME."

"Sorry, that's our five minute lunch break over," the slimer said, as the others started to file out of the room.

"No, wait! Don't go back to work. That's Grek's voice. She's from Andromeda!"

"We know," the slimer said. "But there's nothing we can do."

"There is! We could all go to the palace together and–"

"BING BONG! ALL YOU NEED IS SLIME!" said the loudspeaker.

The slimers all left. They had given up resisting Grek and just did everything she said. I would have to go the palace alone and find Holly. But there was something else I needed to do first.

It was time for another important moment: I was going to disobey my parents for the very first time. I'd only just found them – there was no way I was going to leave them behind like they'd asked.

I thrust my hand back through the tunnel which was now a large crack. They were still there. Carefully folding my fingers around them, I scooped up Mum and Dad.

9

TURNS OUT UPRISINGS ARE SURPRISINGLY FUN

Lifting them out, I opened up my palm so Mum and Dad could breathe.

"It's been so long, I can't remember how to tell him off, can you?" Dad asked Mum.

"I don't think we ever did," Mum said.

"I couldn't just leave you in those horrible tunnels," I explained. "We're in this together."

Mum and Dad turned to each other, and from what I had – impressively quickly – learned about slug body language, they exchanged a look of quiet pride.

"Listen, how do we get out of here?"

"Just take any tunnel that goes up," Dad said.

It was obvious when he put it like that.

We made our way through the tunnels, passing the slimers who were now back at work scraping the walls with their hands.

"Come with me," I begged them.

"It's no use," Mum said sadly. "They only obey Grek's voice. They know their families will suffer otherwise. The mine used to be a happy place where slime was harvested for all. Now they're just slaves."

As if to illustrate her point, the speaker blared out again. "BING BONG! SLIMERS HAVE REALLY STRONG BLADDERS AND DON'T NEED ANY TOILET BREAKS AT ALL."

I stopped walking suddenly and Mum lurched to the side, nearly falling off my hand.

"Don't kill your mother," Dad said sharply.

"Sorry. I've just seen something," I explained.

"That's no excuse for matricide."

We were nearly at the entrance, and I'd spotted a small locked room with a window. I could see what looked like recording equipment inside. "I wonder. Mum or Dad – do you think you can get in there?"

Dad nodded and I bent down to pop him on the floor. He oozed under the door and about ten minutes later I heard a button beep and the door slowly opened.

"Quick, wasn't I?" he wheezed.

Inside a machine was whirring away. It looked just like Bill's old tape recorder that he sometimes let me get down from the attic so I could make The Jasper Show (the best radio show ever starring DJ Jasper and a series of reluctant guests, mostly Holly). I slipped into the room and popped my parents on a desk where they looked around with interest.

"BING BONG! SLIMERS DON'T NEED HOLIDAYS. THEY PREFER TO WORK EXTRA HARD FOR TWO WEEKS INSTEAD."

On the machine were buttons just like Bill's tape recorder. I pressed what I thought looked like stop.

"BING B–"

A drawer shot out and plonked something that looked like a small cassette into my hand. I threw it on the ground and stamped on it, and when that didn't do anything I pulled out the ribbon. I threw the resulting mangled mess into the bin, and then pulled off my green boiler suit and helmet and chucked them in as well.

"Ha! No more stupid slogans," I said, pulling my woolly hat out of my pocket and putting it back on my head. Now I felt like myself again.

"That's my boy!" Dad cheered.

"He's very unpredictable, isn't he?" Mum said. "Must be the green hair."

"Maybe I could even make a new announcement!" I searched through the stuff on the desk. There was a box with some new-looking cassette-like things in it. I put one in and played about until a red recording light came on. There was even a microphone all ready to use.

I took a seat and prepared myself. I would have to do an impression of Grek. Well, that wouldn't be difficult. I had heard her voice going on and on about how amazing Andromeda was enough times. Plus I was famous at school for my impression of Mrs Pardew. "The bell is for me, not for you," was my most popular phrase. I even did a pretty good Mary, but only behind her back. I cleared my throat.

"BING BONG! GREK HERE, THE SLIMY SLIME MINSTER OF GLOOP. WHAT'S THE DIFFERENCE BETWEEN ME AND SLIME? THAT'S RIGHT, NOTHING! AND TO CELEBRATE THAT, TODAY IS A HOLIDAY. SO HAVE A FUN DAY AND COME OVER TO THE PALACE WHERE I AM PRETENDING TO BE THE RULER AND HELP YOURSELVES TO ANYTHING YOU WANT AS A NICE REWARD! OVER AND OUT!"

"What a lovely thought," Mum said.

I picked Mum and Dad up and we started towards the door, then had to leap back as a tidal wave of slimers came pouring out of the depths of the slime mine and through the tunnel, laughing and chatting. Mum was right – they did everything 'Grek' said and she had now told them to take the day off. We let them go past, and then I popped Mum and Dad in my pocket so I didn't drop them and followed the slimers outside. I hadn't thought it would work so well. In fact, I hadn't thought of anything, I'd just said the first thing that came into my head. As usual.

"You really should clean out those pockets," Dad said, choking on a piece of fluff as I lifted him and Mum out and we stood under the dazzling light of three suns.

"How long has it been since these trousers were washed?" Mum asked.

"I don't know. Weeks? Now what do I do?" I asked, watching the slimers hurrying away, whooping and patting each other on the back.

"Now you go the palace and claim your throne," Dad said. "Time to do what you were born to do. Time to become the Slime King."

"But you're the Slime King."

"Not any more. We've been slugs for too long. We're happy with who we are."

Mum nodded. "We just love the lifestyle. No stress. Saves me a fortune in colouring books."

"But I'm not a king. I'm just a boy with green hair."

"That is a king round here," Dad said firmly. "Now pop us down and go and claim your kingdom. It's really unpleasant being ferried around in those pockets of yours."

"I'll come back for you," I promised, placing them carefully on a smooth stone.

We said our goodbyes for the second time and I walked away, a tear in my eye and a lump in my throat. Then I ran back and shoved them in my pocket again. They were my long lost parents – I wasn't about to leave them at the side of the road next to an abandoned slime mine. Besides, I still hadn't asked them where my strange and embarrassing middle name came from. Or how much pocket money they were going to give me.

Could it be backdated, even? These were things I needed to know.

I caught up with the slimers and we marched back to the city together. The further they got from the slime mine, the more cheerful they became. They couldn't believe Grek had granted them a day's holiday. And so it was that I arrived at the Royal Palace of Gloop at the head of an army of slimers, fired up and ready to have fun. Lots of fun. They hadn't had fun since Andromeda had taken over their galaxy ten years ago.

The palace was beautiful, if you liked the colour green a lot. Luckily I did.

"Wow," I breathed as we approached the fancy gates carved in the shape of Mum and Dad holding me as a baby. Bit weird.

"Who goes there?" demanded a guard, dressed in a tall, green hat and holding what looked like a giant water gun. "A load of slimy old slimers, is it?" He jabbed his weapon at us. "Get out of here, go on!"

I heard Dad clear his throat in my pocket, so I quickly palmed him and put him to my ear in case he had any sage words of advice.

"How dare you!" Dad said.

"Oh, sorry, Dad."

Dad let out an exasperated sigh. "No, you say that to him."

"Oh, right. Erm… How dare you! I am the Slime Prince, the long lost heir to the throne, and this is my avenging army."

I whipped off my hat, to the accompaniment of gasps of surprise from the slimers.

"Hasn't changed much, has he?" one of the slimers at the front commented, pointing to the real me and the me on the gates.

The guard looked confused. "Something's up. I'm telling the Slime Minister."

"We'll tell her ourselves," I said boldly. "To the palace!"

I raised my arm and, to my surprise, the slimers obeyed me and charged past the guard, pushing open the gate and sweeping me up with them. We hurtled towards the palace with whoops and cheers. Running up a set of grand stairs, we passed through a massive door and found ourselves in a huge hall set out like a museum, with loads of weird artefacts on shelves and pedestals.

"Oh no! Grek's turned the palace into a giant Andromedan display cabinet!" Mum wailed from my hand. "And I'd just redecorated too."

As she spoke, two slimers picked up a twisted vase and started chucking it to each other with gales of laughter. Several others jumped up and began walking along the shelves, sending ornaments and antiques scattering. The rest spotted the banisters and were soon sliding down them like bobsleigh teams. Those slimers had ten years' worth of fun built up inside them and they were going to let it out no matter what.

"Don't worry, Mum. Most of that stuff will be broken in a few minutes. Now, which way to the dungeons? We have to rescue Holly."

"This is our home! We've never had dungeons," Mum said, appalled.

Dad cleared his throat nervously. "Well, actually…"

"Oh, darling!"

"Just a few, just in case. For really bad people. I never used them," Dad added quickly.

Mum sighed. "And you think you know someone."

But before we could go anywhere, there was a loud out-of-tune fanfare from the entrance we had just come through that was horribly familiar. Most of the slimers ran off up the stairs, laughing as they continued their trail of joyful destruction. I shoved Mum and Dad back in my pocket before they could protest and ducked behind a huge statue of the giant spiky purple dictator Emperor Iko Iko Iko – just in time. Two guards marched in, each carrying a pole on which was slung a giant hammock, and on the giant hammock was slung a giant spiky purple dictator.

"All hail Iko Iko Iko, son of Iko Iko and grandson of Iko, Emperor of Andromeda Galaxy. That's Iko Iko Iko who's the Emperor, not the grandad although he was one too but now he's not coz he's dead," said a bored guard before being slapped in the face.

WHACK!

"It's him!" I whispered. "The real version of this." I pointed to the statue of the Emperor that we were hiding behind.

"If you're pointing to something, don't bother," came Dad's muffled voice. "We can't see a thing in here."

"Sorry."

"Quiet!" Mum hissed.

I did what Mum said (though the novelty was beginning to wear off a bit) and stayed hidden as the Emperor was carried further into the hall.

"All hail Iko Iko Iko, Your Emperorship, Your Majesty!" Grek said in a rush, bustling out with her cloak flying behind her and her pointy eyebrows almost coming off the top of her head. "We've had an emergency. With some slimers. They're everywhere!"

"So I see," the Emperor boomed as two slimers dashed past throwing a pottery urn between them like a rugby ball.

"That's priceless!" Grek screamed. "You mindless idiots! That's the commemorative urn celebrating my first six months as que–I mean, as temporary ruling minister on behalf of Andromeda! Bing bong, back to work! Why don't my announcements work anymore?"

I grinned to myself. The slimers were finally learning to disobey Grek.

"Have you completely lost control of this galaxy, Grek?" the Emperor rumbled. "I thought you said you could handle it?"

"I could! I can! I got rid of the royal family, didn't I? And I enslaved loads of the citizens by making them work in the mine–"

She stopped as another group of slimers rushed

past, four of them this time. They were having great fun chucking a bust of Grek to each other. It had glasses and a moustache drawn on it. "You catch this ugly mug," one of them was yelling.

"So I see," the Emperor said slowly. "And to think I was considering asking you to run another Solar System for me as well. Never mind. I already had my doubts. I have a replacement for you already lined up."

"But – you can't replace me!" Grek protested.

"True," the Emperor agreed.

"Oh thank you, your mighty Emperorship Majesty!" Grek gasped, throwing herself on the floor in gratitude.

"No, you haven't given us any refreshments yet," the Emperor continued. "After that you'll be completely expendable." He puffed out his spines. "To the great feasting room! You do have a great feasting room, don't you?"

Grek scrambled up, gave a terrified nod and hurried miserably off, the guards following with the

Emperor on his hammock between them.

I fished Mum and Dad out and we all looked at each other with dismay.

"This is worse than I thought," said Dad. "The Emperor, here?"

"And the place looks such a mess," Mum added in despair.

"What shall I do?" I asked.

Dad dipped his antennae. "Over to you, son."

Mum did the same. "Whatever you do, we're with you."

She was right about that. I popped them back in my pocket and tiptoed after the others. They had gone into a big throne room. There were loads of murals on the wall of Grek giving speeches to huge crowds and offering sage advice to grateful ancient slimers. It was truly nauseating.

The Emperor's guards tipped him onto the throne which disappeared under his spiny blubber, making it look like he was floating just above the ground.

Grek bowed low in front of him. "I have ordered

refreshments for you of course, Your Imperial Majesticness. But before you consider the small matter of my life, you might be pleased to hear that I recently recaptured an old prisoner of yours, the heir to the very throne you are crushing – I mean, sitting on – now."

The Emperor glowered. "And you brought him back to Triangulum? Then I certainly will be killing you. Followed by him."

I gulped and reached into my pocket for reassurance. I was hiding behind another statue of the Emperor. (How many more could there be? But at least they offered plenty of shelter.) Mum and Dad pressed their slimy heads against my hand, giving me courage. Then the door behind me swung open and in came, of all people, Holly.

She had her hair tied back and wore a smart red jacket, and was carrying a cushion with a plate of weird-looking food on it. She nearly dropped the lot when she saw me.

Jasper? she mouthed. *Are you okay?*

I nodded and did a thumbs up to show I was fine. Questions crowded my head but I bit them all back. She widened her eyes and gave me a look. Years of being *looked* at by Holly allowed me to decipher the meaning instantly.

I melted back behind the statue and watched as Holly approached the throne.

"You ordered refreshments, Slime Minister."

"Ah," Grek said. "My new slave. After you, Your Spineyness."

"Hmm." The Emperor didn't move. "How do I know you're not trying to poison me?"

"As if I would try to poison you, Your Majestic Triple Emperorness! Here, I'll prove it." Grek went to grab something small and slimy off the plate. I saw Holly spin the plate around so Grek took a particularly brightly coloured blob, which she stuffed in her mouth. Instantly she started choking.

"Oh," she said in a strangulated voice. "It appears that I was."

10
TURNS OUT SOMEONE'S A SECRET AGENT

The next few minutes were very awkward as everyone stood and watched Grek choking. Not one person helped, even some slimers who had come in to play football with a giant diamond. Finally she lay on the floor, unconscious.

"That was nicely done," the Emperor said calmly. "Who poisoned the food, slave?"

Holly chucked the cushion and the rest of the food over her shoulder. "Me, actually. She's not really dead. It's a Gloop sleeping herb that just knocks you out for a bit. But she deserves it. She stole the throne. The real king is over there, behind that statue of you. The one on the left."

This was awful. Holly was unwittingly turning me over to the Emperor! But how was she to know the Emperor was my mortal enemy who had kidnapped me as a baby? It wasn't as though either of us were wearing a badge.

"Who is that?" the Emperor barked out. "Come here or I'll have you zapped!"

"Be brave, son," Dad whispered.

With shaking legs, I came out of my hiding place and walked up a long, green carpet towards the Emperor and his guards. I patted my pocket. I would keep Mum and Dad safe no matter what. And I would be brave. Well, for as long as I could manage anyway.

"Hello, Your Triple Yuckiness," I said, approaching the throne. "Turns out I'm the rightful ruler of this place, not you. So you can get your big lardy jelly bottom out of my throne and back to Andromeda smartish."

I heard tiny muffled cheering coming from my pocket, and then the Emperor's guards grabbed me and twisted my hands behind my back.

"Let him go, you big bully!" Holly yelled.

"Oh, okay!" the Emperor said in a fake weedy voice, pretending to be scared. Then he went back to his usual bellow. "Guards! Take them to the dungeons until I can decide what to do with them."

"Er, which one?" the guard holding me asked.

"Both of them, of course!"

"No, I mean which guard?"

"The answer is the same, you knuckleheads!" the Emperor screeched.

WHACK! His slapping hand nearly walloped me as well.

"Do it now, son," Mum called.

"Yes, go on son. Do it now," Dad echoed.

"What?" I twisted round to try and get my ear nearer to my pocket, which isn't easy when you're being held by an alien guard and aren't a contortionist.

"Get them down to the dungeons before I zap you myself!" the Emperor seethed.

Then I realised what Mum meant, and I did it.

I changed myself into a slug.

Let me stop here and just say that changing into a slug is not easy. First of all you have to stop being a human, and that's hard. Though I guess it's easier for me as I'm an alien. And that's just the first step. There are seven in total. Seven steps to becoming a slug. Which is ironic as slugs only have one foot. Taking seven steps is a big deal to them. Anyway, I worked through them and this time it was actually a little bit easier because I'd done it before. I even managed to do the tail last this time, instead of first.

When the process was complete I looked round for Mum and Dad, hoping to see their big friendly sluggy faces next to me as I'd flung them out of my pocket just before doing the whole slug changing thing. Phew, there they were.

Only they were small. Just as small as they had been before. And everyone else was the same size as they had been before, too.

"Sorry," I said to Holly. "I tried something but it

didn't work."

Holly was staring at me. So was everyone else. The guards were backing away from me in disgust. The Emperor's little hands were up in dismay and he was struggling to speak.

"Something's worked all right," Holly said. "Well, it's either worked or gone horribly wrong. What exactly were you trying to do?"

"Turn myself into a slug?"

"You are a slug," Holly said. "A four foot six slug. I'd get you a mirror so you can see yourself but I don't think there's one big enough."

I looked down. Holly was right. Everything about me was slug. Everything except the size. I was a human-sized slug.

"You missed out step seven," Dad called up helpfully.

"Yes, thanks Dad. I realised that when Holly said I was a four foot six slug."

"Did you just say 'Dad' to that slug down there?" Holly's eyes were round. I would have said they

were out on stalks, but that was *my* eyes.

"Oh. Yes. I'd better introduce you. This is Holly, my foster sister. Holly, these are my parents."

I gently lifted up Mum and Dad with my tail.

"Lovely to meet you," they squealed.

"When you've quite finished!" the Emperor yelled.

I'd almost forgotten he was there in all the slug-related excitement. Problem was, my plan had been to change into a tiny slug and escape. Now I was a giant slug, that wasn't going to happen. It was a stupid plan anyway because it would have left Holly at the mercy of old Spinychops on the throne over there, but at least it would have been something.

"Sorry. Looks like we're going to the dungeons after all," I said as one of the guards tried to get hold of me.

"Yuck, he's all slimy and disgusting, Your Triple Iko-ness," the guard said, recoiling. "Eeewwww!"

"Don't be pathetic. Grab him!" the Emperor shouted, bulging with anger.

The other guard let go of Holly and reached out for a wad of slug flesh. I squirmed away, squirting out some slime to slide along on. The guard looked like he was on an invisible bicycle as his legs flailed around trying to keep him upright.

Slime! Of course! That was my superpower!

"Come and get me," I called, oozing away as quickly as I could and leaving a slimy trail on the floor. Both guards lunged after me and fell flat on their faces. Holly hooted with laughter, then started slipping and sliding herself.

"Get behind me Hols!" I called out, moving to shelter Mum and Dad. "I'm going to blast him!"

By 'him', I meant Iko Iko Iko, son of Iko Iko, grandson of Iko, Emperor of Andromeda and future ruler of the Milky Way once the paperwork was done. But basically a big ball of spines on a badly fitting throne.

"You think you can defeat me?" he bellowed. "Zap him, zap him, zap him!"

The guards were still on the floor. Every time

they tried to stand up, they fell over.

I smiled a small, satisfied sluggy smile.

"How about I zap you for a change, blubberchops?" I said, and blasted him in the face. Slime dripped down into his eyes and he let out a yell of rage.

"Sorry about that. I meant to do this." My next jet of slime was much better. It knocked him off the throne and threw him across the room where he stuck to the back wall, his spines handily piercing a mural of Grek (striding across Gloop watched by an adoring crowd) and pinning him to the wall.

"Good shot, son!" Dad cried.

"I'm so proud!" Mum sobbed.

Grek started to wake up. Unfortunately Holly was right, she wasn't dead after all.

"What's going on?" she mumbled, taking in the scene of slimy carnage. Then she noticed the Emperor embedded in the wall. She gasped with horror. "And what's happened to my mural?"

"Oh, hello Grek. It's complicated."

"Probably easier just to show her," Holly suggested.

"You're right," I agreed, and gave her a good squirt of slime. Soon she was back on the floor in a pool of slime, just like the two guards.

Holly folded her arms and looked me up and down. "Well, look at you. Shall I even ask, or just accept the massive improvement in your looks?"

"It's my heritage."

"Technically it's more of an allergy," Dad called up.

I quickly filled Holly in about being kidnapped by Grek and meeting my parents in the slime mines. She accepted it all straight away, which was a big leap considering she'd refused to believe Flarp was an alien just a few days ago.

"What about you?" I asked.

"Well, I–" Holly stopped and snorted. "Sorry, it's just so weird trying to talk normally when you're a giant slug."

"Wait a minute, I'll change back." I started step

155

seven, remembered I hadn't done that the first time round, then went to step six. Nothing happened. I skipped to step five, but that wasn't getting anything going either. "I'll do it in a minute. We might need more slime anyway. So go on."

"Well, when you disappeared on me I thought I might as well go with the other servants to the palace. When I asked where my room was going to be, everyone just laughed and showed me a corner of the kitchen floor. I wasn't having that, so I told the servants who I was and who you were. They were really excited to hear the Slime Prince had come home, even though I told them you're just my bogey-brain brother. Then they told me all about Grek and how mean and horrible she is, but how they were too frightened to disobey her as she had all their relatives working in the slime mines like slaves. Well I wasn't having that either, so I got them to use all their cookery skills to make something that would stop Grek from being such a pain in the bum."

"I can hear you, you know," Grek said, choking on a bit of slime.

"Good," Holly said. "Now, Your Slugness, how do we dispose of this lot?"

"Perhaps," said a smooth voice, like chocolate melting on the tongue, "I can help."

A tall, vomitingly good-looking young man skidded into the room, halting with a smooth glide. He had floppy curly hair, a smart suit and a face straight from Holly's t-shirt. A guitar was slung across his back.

"Oh. My. God. It's him! It's you! It's Harry Handsome!" Holly swooned. I pushed her back upright with my tail.

"That's right, babe, it's me, Harry Handsome." Harry rearranged his carefully tousled head of curls. "Well, that's what I call myself when I'm doing my secret agent undercover work on Earth."

"A secret agent! I knew you were so much more than just a fabulously good-looking pop star." Holly batted her eyelids. "So, what do you call yourself

157

the rest of the time, Mr Handsome?"

"Actually I still use that name the rest of the time as well. Kind of suits me, doesn't it?"

I pretended to barf but Holly didn't notice.

Even Mum was giggling like a little girl. "What a nice looking young man. And so well brought up."

"How can you be undercover when you're a famous pop star?" I scoffed.

"You can't hide talent," Harry said with a wink. "I was there to find the heir to Gloop and bring him home."

"Well you didn't try very hard," I grumbled.

"I've had a very hectic tour schedule, not to mention a Pop Heart-Throbs photo session." Harry struck a pose and I actually heard Holly sigh. "Hey, maybe you guys can help me. Even you, giant slug. I'm looking for someone named Jasper."

It was the final straw. I readied my slime blasters.

"No!" Holly shrieked. "You'll ruin his hair!"

"Yeah," Harry agreed. "Mind the 'do, man."

Reluctantly I gave in and spared him the slime.

"I'm Jasper. I'm the heir to Gloop. I found myself. At least, I think I did."

"That makes sense. I didn't realise I was looking for a giant slug. Well, seems you took care of everything yourselves." He nodded at the Emperor, Grek and the two guards who were still struggling in the slime. The more they struggled the more tangled up they got. "Still, maybe there's something I can do. I know, the gift of music. I'll do an impromptu acoustic set for the slimers. That'll keep their spirits up. See you later, Harry fans."

"He's so giving!" Holly cried, as Harry flicked his hair at us and slid expertly away on a thin layer of slime.

Soon the cheesy riffs of his smash hit 'You Will Always Love Me (And I Don't Blame You)' filled the palace.

"I thought he was going to help them, not torture them," I said.

I put my head out of the door. A lot of the slimers were already leaving, some of them covering their

159

ears.

"What is that blasted racket?" one was saying.

"I dunno. And what are we doing here, in the palace?"

"Ain't got a clue. Tell you what, let's go home and have our slime pasties."

Looked like the brain washing was wearing off. Probably a good thing.

I returned to Holly. At least she would see what an idiot Harry was now.

"Wow." Holly sunk onto the throne, fanning herself. "I *knew* he was out of this world with cheekbones like that. Top pop star *and* galactic secret agent. And to think he was only on Earth to find my stinky little brother." Her brows lowered in sudden annoyance. "If you hadn't run away, he would have found us. Me and him could have been an item by now. You ruin everything."

I turned to Mum and Dad to share a shrug but they were swaying back and forth to the distant guitar chords.

"Beautiful words," Dad said. "The sort of lyrics that mean something to everyone."

I sighed heavily. "Never mind Harry Heavesome, we need to deal with these four." I pointed my tail at what I now collectively thought of as 'The Baddies'. Emperor Iko Iko Iko was still embedded in the wall, and Grek and the guards had given up struggling to get up and were sitting there miserably soaked in slime. "Looks like you lot will be seeing the dungeons after all."

"Yes, about those dungeons…" Dad piped up.

"Quiet, darling. I'm missing the chorus," Mum said, closing her eyes to concentrate on the music. Or should I say, 'music'.

11

TURNS OUT SOMEONE'S
A SECRET, SECRET AGENT

Holly helped me push Grek and the guards together and I bound them with another load of slime.

"Couldn't do this as a baby either, could I?" I told Grek jauntily.

"No," Grek sighed. "I preferred you then."

The next thing to do was detach the Emperor from where his spines were sticking into the sickening mural of Grek.

"Keep your horrible human hands off me!" the Emperor rumbled at Holly. "Guards! Zap them!"

We decided to just ignore him. "It must be horrible being in a bad mood all the time," Holly said as she helped me pull out the spines. I did a double take at her but she didn't seem to realise.

We bundled the Emperor over to the others. The best way to do this was by rolling him. And while we rolled him he told us all the things that he'd like to do to us once he was free. Zapping was the main one, followed by blasting and splatting. We bound him up with the others. This slime was brilliant stuff! I was getting good at making it do pretty much anything I wanted.

"Right. Let's get this lot to where they belong."

Turns out I didn't need Holly's help. As a giant slug I not only had super slime but super strength. Holly carried Mum and Dad while I followed Dad's directions and bundled the baddies across the main hall. The floor was now littered with broken Andromedan artefacts and bits of Grek and the Emperor that were once statues.

"Look! There's Grek's eyebrow!" I said excitedly, spotting a small triangular piece of marble on the floor.

Grek let out an angry sob. The Emperor continued to describe how we would be thoroughly splatted.

The guards were a bit more relaxed. "This floor could do with a bit of a sweep," one said.

"You're not wrong there," said the other.

I guess they were used to being mistreated and just took it for granted.

Dad directed us to an old wooden door and I pushed the villains down some steps and into the deep, dark, disgusting dungeons – or so I had expected.

"What a lovely airy room!" Mum exclaimed as we emerged into a comfortable lounge. Squishy sofas were set around a giant TV screen. Bowls of snacks and dips sat on a small table. There was a table tennis table at the far end.

"That's what I was trying to tell you," Dad said. "I knew I'd never use it for prisoners so I thought, why not make it into a nice, er…"

"Man den?" Mum said.

"Well yes, I suppose it is really. But I only came down here when the strain of ruling got really bad."

Mum leaned against him. "I think it's lovely. Hold us up a bit higher, would you Holly love?"

I was able to melt the slime bonds by flicking them with my tail. The Emperor and Grek fell gratefully into the two squishy sofas. The guards had a quick look round and then ambled over to the table tennis table where they began warming up.

"Great. We've sentenced them to a life of luxury."

"Not complete luxury, son," Dad said. "They have to share a kitchen and bathroom."

"Anyone else want to play Round the World?" one of the guards said, holding up some table tennis bats. "No? Just us then, mate."

Grek had recovered herself and stood up. "You're not leaving me here with him!" she fumed, pointing at the Emperor.

The Emperor tried to stand up, but couldn't. Perhaps he'd never had to use his own feet before.

165

"How dare you, you insignificant Triangulum scum! I made you everything you are! Or should I say, were!"

"Are!"

"Were!"

"Are!"

"Were!"

"Shall we leave them to it?" Holly suggested.

We sneaked out while they were arguing and Dad told me where he hid the dungeon key (under the 'Welcome' mat). I turned it and locked them in with immense satisfaction. I didn't have a clue what I was going to do with them, but at least they were out of the way for now. I hoped they could find a good film to watch that wouldn't make them argue too much.

"Well done, son," Dad said from Holly's hand as we walked upstairs, or in my case, oozed. "Your first act as Slime King has freed many galaxies from oppression."

"Are you sure you don't want the job, Dad?" I asked him.

"Not a jot! Now you're back, I'm officially retired. We're going to be full-time slugs, aren't we darling?"

"Wonderful," agreed Mum.

We reached the grand entrance hall. It was quiet and empty. Seemed like the slimers had moved on somewhere else to enjoy the rest of their day off. Or they'd simply had enough of Harry Handsome's sickly lyrics. There was no sound coming from his guitar anymore either, thank goodness. The 'concert' must have finished.

"If I've missed getting Harry's autograph, I'm blaming you, slug face," Holly said.

"Technically that's not an insult. It's a fact," I told her, but she had already popped Mum and Dad down on an empty plinth and dashed off in search of her hero.

As soon as she had gone, I squished down beside them. A knot of nerves and doubt had been growing inside me. "Mum. Dad. I don't know if I can do this," I confessed. My voice echoed around the hall.

"I don't know anything about slime or being a king. I'd be the worst slime king in the history of slime kings."

"All you have to do," Dad said, "is look after your subjects."

"It's very easy," Mum added. "Grek's made them all slaves in the slime mines, so you don't have to do anything. Just sit back and enjoy the money rolling in."

"What!" I was shocked. I'd quite liked my new mum up until now. "I couldn't do that! I'd pay proper wages, improve the conditions, serve crinkle-cut chips in the canteen and help people who don't want to work with slime do other jobs instead like, I don't know, accountancy."

Mum beamed. "I told you he'd do a good job, darling."

Phew. She wasn't evil after all, just testing me. Parents were obviously a bit tricky like that.

"But how do I protect everyone from the rest of Andromeda? Won't they want to get revenge now we're holding their Emperor captive?"

"Oh, don't worry about them," Dad said. "They all hate His Triple Weirdness. Now he's our prisoner, we're perfectly safe. In fact, I predict there will never be any more problems in the whole galaxy ever again."

Well, that all sounded good. I stood up with a puff of relief, just as Holly came rushing back in, breathless and tearful.

"Harry Handsome's gone!"

"More good news. Could this day get any better?"

"And so has the Emperor! They took The Big Green Space-Busting Machine."

"You mean – Harry Handsome was working for the other side? He's even more repulsive than I thought," I spat.

"What do you mean?" Holly sniffed.

"He's a double agent, isn't he? He's working for old Spinychops and he's busted him out of the dungeons."

Mum let out a squeak. "How can someone so beautiful be so ghastly?"

"It's not all about looks, you know," Dad said.

"I knew there was something up with him. No one can really be that vacant," I fumed, thrashing my tail.

Mum dashed slowly away from my tail, which had got dangerously close to the plinth they were on. "Careful, darling!"

"Sorry." I tried to keep my tail under control. If you've ever had a tail, you'll understand how hard it was. "But the Emperor's escaped. It was all for nothing."

"Nothing is for nothing," Dad said, confusingly. "What I mean is, you're here and that's the important thing. With a proper ruler, Gloop will be able to stand up for itself again. We can face the Emperor and do our best to protect our galaxy."

I had a whole galaxy to rule, and I couldn't even control my own tail. "Do you think I'll stay a giant slug forever?"

"Can't you change back?" Holly asked, wiping her nose.

I tried again. I even added an extra step seven to the process or, as most people call it, eight. I think that made it worse, actually.

"Not this time," I admitted.

"We love you no matter what you are," Mum said fondly.

"Yes, but you love slugs."

"I quite like you as a slug," Holly said. "It's easier to find ways to insult you."

"I told you, those aren't insults. They're fact-based descriptions."

"You think so, slime-breath?"

"It's probably better this way, son," Dad said. "You'll be more accepted as king. They love anything slimy round here."

"Do you think he'll fit on the throne?" Mum asked anxiously.

"Is there anything left of the throne after the Emperor sat on it?"

We all went off to see. And that was how my reign of Gloop began.

TURNS OUT WE DON'T NEED A CODE GREEN (OR IS IT RED?)

Turns out I could fit on the remains of the throne – just – and, after it was mended, from then on I was Slime King of Gloop. Sounds impressive, doesn't it? Well, the King bit anyway. Don't tell anyone, but it wasn't actually that hard.

Once I'd passed some laws making the slime mines really nice places to work in, with five star canteens, sports clubs and spas, all I had to do was open a few fetes, kiss some babies and settle the odd dispute. With Grek still in the dungeon (Harry Handsome hadn't bothered rescuing her), and no further attacks from the Emperor as yet, Gloop was a peaceful place. Not a beautiful place as it was basically a big ball of slime, but peaceful. And I belonged there. It was my home.

Everything was perfect, but as the weeks went on it felt like there was something missing. Not my arms and legs, although they were too. Something I couldn't put my finger on, even if I had one.

"I sort of wish Grek wasn't in the dungeons," I said to Holly as I struggled to choose which portrait of me should go on the new Gloop One Hundred Ping Note (worth 1p). Should it be giant slug front view or giant slug side view? Would anyone be able to tell the difference? "I'm sure a Slime Minister would have done all this stuff for me."

"Don't be lazy. Anyway, I'm helping you."

I had a brilliant thought. "I could make *you*–"

"No way, slug face." Holly cut me off. "I'm not being anyone's Slime anything." She jabbed a finger at the profile portrait. Both had been painted in slime by a really talented slime artist. "This one looks nobler. But you know what? You might even need a new portrait soon. I think you're turning back."

I twisted round to look at my tail. It definitely looked a bit shorter. And I'd grown some stubby arms! I was like a slug crossed with a T Rex. I was Slug Rex. "About time," I sighed. "How long has it been?"

"Three Earth weeks and four Earth days," Holly said promptly. "I think."

That long? I suddenly felt guilty. It was my fault Holly was here. I'd come because I'd wanted to and because this was my home, but she'd only come to try and keep me out of trouble. I reached out to put a hand on her arm, but gave up as it was too short.

"I never thought. You must be homesick. I'm not, obviously. I live here. How could I be homesick?" I laughed loudly, but it didn't sound like my normal laugh and echoed unpleasantly round the high-ceilinged room.

"I'm definitely not homesick either," Holly said, her voice just as wobbly. "I only remember we've been here that long because that was the last time I saw Harry Handsome. I'm not thinking about home at all."

"That traitor." I bashed my tail on the floor angrily.

"He never said he was on our side to begin with. He just said he'd been sent to Earth to look for you."

"He still committed crimes against music." Unfortunately I hadn't been able to escape Harry's output, even on Gloop. Holly had no access to his songs so she had been singing them to herself instead. Out loud. All the time. "You could go home, Hols. If you wanted."

"And leave you here on your own like a great, big, useless, old slug?"

"I've got Mum and Dad."

"They're living under a stone in the palace vegetable garden. Anyway, I couldn't just go. All the spaceships are on standby in case Emperor Bellyflop launches a revenge attack."

"Do you think he will?"

Holly shrugged. "Who knows, but he is ruler of

Triangulum. And the Milky Way too, once the paperwork's been sorted out."

I gulped. "Do you think he's doing anything to… Earth?"

"Probably not."

"He said it was the jewel of the Solar System."

"People look at jewels. They don't do things to them."

"He's not a person."

"Whatever happens, there's nothing we can do. We've got enough trouble here." Holly looked out of the window. "Look, all three suns are setting at the same time."

Silently, we moved to the window and looked out across the ornamental slime lakes towards the triple sunset. A crowd of slimers had gathered to watch the rare event. I had given them permission to use the grounds of the palace as much as they wanted. It was the only nice place in Gloop, really.

"Nice to see the slimers enjoying themselves–" I began, as they screamed and scattered in every direction.

A spaceship had landed next to the plubber maze. And it wasn't one of ours.

Holly and I looked at each other, and I felt my antennae sticking up in fear.

"The Emperor," I gulped.

"Remember the plan," Holly said.

She was right. We did have a plan. And it involved slime.

I oozed to a corner of the room where a walkie-talkie device connected to my security team downstairs, a small group of slimers who had volunteered for the job because they loved to sleep.

"Security! Wake up! Code green, code green!"

"What's code green again?" a bleary voice asked.

"Load the slime cannons!"

"I thought that was code red."

"It's green. Green for slime."

"I s'pose that does make sense when you think about it."

"Well, can you stop thinking about it and just do

it? Quickly?"

"Whoops. Yes, Your Greenness. At once."

I squidged back towards the window to see if our plan was going to work.

"Stop!" Holly yelled.

"Don't worry, he'll stop when the slime hits him," I said, trying to rub my tiny hands together and finding they didn't reach.

"No, *you* need to stop! It's not the Emperor!"

"What?"

A servant burst in. I had recently promoted him to messenger and he was very keen.

"Your Royal Greenness! A small party has arrived and they are demanding to speak with you. They said their names were Mary and Bill. Oh, and someone called Flarp?"

"Stop the slime cannons, will you?" I called out to the messenger, as Holly and I took one look at each other and began to sprint down the stairs.

Yes, sprint. With my legs.

Because a funny thing happened as I careered

towards the stairs. The more I thought of Mary and Bill, the more human I felt. By the time I got to the bottom, I had a bottom. Plus two legs, two normal-sized arms and a neck. An actual neck. And clothes too!

Not that I paid much attention at the time. All I could think of was getting down those stairs as quickly as possible. I could hear Holly laughing behind me and I was laughing too as we burst through the doors into the throne room.

"His Royal Greenness, the Slime King of Gloop!" the servant announced breathlessly, skidding in after us.

I quickly straightened my face and put on my best kingly manner.

"Welcome to Gloop, strangers," I said regally. "May I help you? Do you need a dispute settled? Or perhaps you'd like me to open a fete?"

It was them. Mary wore a sleek spacesuit and a wide smile. Bill was in a similar outfit but from the nineteen eighties and about four sizes too small.

Flarp wore a floppy hat and sunglasses. She had a little tube round her neck which she kept looking through and pressing. I think she was taking photos.

"What a marvellous place you've got here, Jasper," she said. "The architecture is quite Neptunian."

Mary couldn't hold herself back any longer. "Holly! Jasper!" she shrieked, rushing towards us. She wrapped her arms round both of us. She wouldn't have been able to do that when I was Slug Rex. Bill joined in and the four of us held each other tightly. Inside me, something that had felt empty was suddenly full again.

Holly pulled back first. "Are those legwarmers?"

Bill shrugged. "It's been a long time since I've been in space. But legwarmers never date."

Holly raised an eyebrow. "You tell yourself that if you like, Bill."

Mary prised herself off us and straightened her utility belt. She looked the business, like she should be starring in her own space movie: Mary Versus the

Martians.

"We've been searching for you everywhere. Then we heard a rumour that the Emperor of Andromeda had a new prisoner."

Flarp cut in. "And then, rather amusingly, we found out that the situation had been reversed and the Emperor himself was now the prisoner of his previous victim."

"Not for long," I confessed. "He was busted out by Harry Handsome."

"The good-looking pop musician?" Mary said, shocked.

"Well, one of those things. Anyway, turns out he's an alien secret agent working for Andromeda."

"And to think I'd always assumed it would be someone from the classical side," Flarp mused, crouching down to take an artistic photo of the throne.

"Wait – you knew the Emperor had sent someone after Jasper?" Mary asked.

"My dear, why do you think I was there in the

first place? I was content to watch from afar as it were, and keep in touch with you from time to time, but when Harry Handsome went solo I had my suspicions."

"Yeah, his solo stuff is terrible!" I agreed, before Holly stepped on my foot. "Ouch!"

"Whatever he's done, his hair still looks amazing," Holly said firmly. She looked at Mary and Bill for a moment. "Didn't think you'd come. Thought maybe you'd got fed up with us."

"Fed up with you? We can't get enough of you," Mary said, tears in her eyes, and it was time for another family hugfest.

Flarp waddled over to me. "I'm sorry I didn't protect you adequately, Jasper. To be quite honest, I thought Harry Handsome was too thick to take seriously. And I didn't think you'd run off like that. I also accidentally told you you weren't human, which I suppose led to the running off. In fact, the whole debacle is entirely my fault." Flarp leaned closer. "To tell you the truth, it's not the first time

I've put my oversized orange foot in it, either." She stepped back again. "I want to make it up to you. Whatever I can do to be of service to Gloop and Your Greenness, I will."

Flarp bowed, and then Mary and Bill bowed too, which felt weird considering they'd just been hugging the life out of me a minute before. Holly didn't, obviously.

The regal mood was spoiled by my stomach rumbling loudly. "Who's hungry?" I asked.

Bill clapped his hands. "Great. I've missed sampling exotic food from other galaxies."

"Better lower your expectations, Bill," Holly warned.

"What do you mean?"

"Well, you know all that slime out there? Soon some of it's going to be in here." She tapped her stomach.

"Lovely," Mary said faintly.

13

TURNS OUT HOME IS WHEREVER YOU WANT IT TO BE

I ordered the nicest slime-based drinks and snacks that we had – not that I wanted them to be slime-based but that's how everything was on Gloop – and we settled down on some giant slime-filled cushions brought in by the enthusiastic servant. As we ate, I filled them in on the whole slime-centric story.

When I got to the part about voting for the Milky Way to be merged with Andromeda, Mary was livid.

"How dare he claim there was no vote from Earth? I sent my postal vote weeks ago, the moment I found out the meeting clashed with my book group."

"You should register a formal complaint immediately," Flarp said, licking her fingers. She was the only one who was actively enjoying the slime. Everyone else was just being polite. "He'll still be sorting out the paperwork at this stage anyway."

Holly and I looked at each other with cautious relief.

"You mean, it won't happen after all?" I asked.

"Not for now. He'll try again next year though. He always does."

"And I'll keep voting against him," Mary said firmly. "He won't get away with it."

"Wow." I was impressed. Every year, it seemed, Mary saved the Earth from an alien invasion. And I'd thought she was boring.

"Go on then," Bill said. "What happened next?"

I told them about trying to vote myself, being spotted by Grek and zooming off to Gloop. When I got to the bit about my real parents being slugs, I could see Mary and Bill trying their best not to look surprised. And when I got to the bit about turning into a slug myself, I wanted to award them an Oscar for Best Performance in Trying To Look Normal While Hearing Something Completely Bizarre. Flarp, of course, was unfazed. I guess she had seen this sort of thing before.

I carried on until all the slime shakes had been slurped and there wasn't a single slimy nugget left in the family slime bucket.

"So let me get this straight," Bill said, popping a slime doughnut into his mouth and then quickly popping it out again. "Your biological parents are in... the vegetable patch?"

"They don't want to be rulers," I explained. "They just want to ooze about eating leaves now. They're retired."

"Don't talk to me about retirement," Flarp complained. "Mine's been one big yawn-fest from start to finish so far. I was hoping for a bit of action here with everyone kidnapping each other but no, it looks like I'll have to send my special attack fleet home."

"Special attack fleet?" I repeated.

Flarp pointed out of the window. A fleet of sleek fighter ships hovered above the lake in an arrow formation.

"Flarp called in a few favours," Mary said.

Flarp patted Mary on the arm. "Anything to help an old friend."

Mary chuckled. "Do you remember when we were nitrogen surfing on Bubel VI and you fell through a black hole and nearly got spaghettified?"

"Good times," Flarp sighed happily.

The anecdotes had started again, but this time I didn't mind a bit.

"Maybe you and your attack fleet could hang around for a bit," I suggested to Flarp when I could squeeze a word into the conversation. "You know, just in case old Spiny Face decides to show up again."

"Maybe we could hang around for a bit too," Bill said.

"If His Greenness says it's okay," Mary added with a smile.

Mary and Bill ended up staying for a whole Gloop week, which was quite a lot longer than an Earth one. So did Flarp and her attack fleet, thank Slime. (I was picking up the Gloop lingo nicely.) Turns out Flarp knew Gloop very well, revealing it was her third favourite slime-covered planet which apparently was praise indeed.

I gave them a guided tour, although there wasn't really much to see. The Great Slime Canyon was a great big canyon full of slime, and the Slime River spoke for itself. Mary and Bill nodded politely at everything but Flarp was really enthusiastic.

"Marvellous, simply marvellous," she told me as we watched Mary and Bill pretending to enjoy taking photos of Mount Slime. "You must be thrilled to be back in your real home."

I didn't answer, and when Flarp asked me what

was wrong I told her what I hadn't been able to tell anyone else. Especially not my parents.

Flarp patted me on the arm. "I have an idea."

Flarp told everyone her idea that night over slimeghetti bolognese in the great hall. Even Mum and Dad came and sat on a tall pile of plubber leaves, slowly descending to the table as they happily munched their way through them.

"I've been thinking," Flarp said, slurping up an extra long strand of slimeghetti. "Since Jasper and Holly haven't finished their schooling, why don't they return to Earth for a while with Mary and Bill? In the meantime, I'll stay here and act as ruler on Jasper's behalf, until he feels ready to return and take over. My fleet will also stay and help protect Gloop from Andromeda and any revenge attacks by the Emperor."

"But what about your retirement?" Bill asked.

"Ah, well. Such a pity that the retirement flat in Bournemouth fell through," Flarp said with a wink in my direction. "Besides, I've realised that although retirement suits some, it isn't really for me. I need something to occupy me. Keeping tabs on an evil emperor will be a nice little hobby. Plus I can always visit the dungeons for a game of table tennis if I get really bored. Apparently Grek's backhand top spin has to be seen to be believed these days."

Mary looked at me. "That's very kind of you, Flarp, but this is Jasper's home. If he wants to stay here, he can."

"What about me?" Holly interrupted. "Don't I get a choice?"

"Holly, you're from Earth. You've had a nice holiday but basically you have to come back and attend Little Blanding Secondary School or Bill and I will go to prison."

"It's not fair!" Holly wailed.

I took a deep breath. "I think I'd like to go home. I mean, to Earth. I mean, wherever."

Mary suppressed a smile. Bill didn't manage to and punched the air. "Yes! I mean, good decision, Jasper."

Flarp stretched out her arms towards the stars. "You're a space citizen now, Jasper," she said. "Home is wherever you want it to be."

Now that Flarp's fighting fleet were here, Gloop's spaceships were free and the next day we set off in one of them for Earth. Sadly the Big Green Space-Busting Machine had been nicked by Harry Handsome but Gloop's own ships were pretty cool, even if they didn't have slime baths. The hardest part of leaving Gloop was saying goodbye to Mum and Dad, but they said they would visit soon and even mentioned a plan to make their own slug-sized spaceship out of pongo leaves. It seemed unlikely, but then everything about Mum and Dad was unlikely.

Mind you, Mary and Bill were turning out to be pretty surprising people too. Not only did Bill fly us back himself but we stopped at Uranus (currently rebranded Planet Posterior) so they could re-enact their first meeting on the Twin Cheeks mountain range. It was pretty embarrassing, but also pretty cool at the same time.

Our first glimpse of Earth from the spaceship was amazing. It looked so colourful compared to the slimy brownness of Gloop and I felt my stomach lurch with emotion. Turns out that was just Bill doing a loop-the-loop to celebrate, and soon we were all tumbling about and bumping into each other. Well, Holly and I were. Mary was right of course: we should have put on our seatbelts.

Being back on Earth was a bit weird at first. I actually felt taller and wondered if it was because I was now a King and had a regal bearing. But Holly said it was because gravity was weaker on Gloop and I'd soon be a short barf-brain again just like normal. (She was wrong. Bill measured me a month later and I'd grown an inch. A whole inch!)

It also felt weird because I was constantly on the lookout for the Emperor, in case he came to Earth to get his revenge. Bill said the best thing to do in these cases was to get on with your life and deal with disaster when or if it ever came. And he knows about these things.

So I went back to school, played football with Chad, Max, Charlie, Ali and Jake in Little Blanding Park and did all the other things I used to do before I knew I was a Slime King. I even went back into Asbi's. I couldn't resist checking out the self-service checkout, but it had yellow and black warning tape all over it and was out of order. I slipped out again before the cashier could recognise me.

Not long after we got back, Mary and Bill called a Family Meeting in the kitchen. The first thing I saw when I went in there was a triple layer chocolate cake. In fact that was the only thing I saw as I didn't have eyes for anything else until Mary (apparently she was there too) cut me a slice.

"Well," Bill said. (He was there as well, I realised, and Holly.) "After our latest adventures, Mary and I have decided we're not going to have any more secrets from you."

Mary helped herself to cake. She always took her slice last, a trait I greatly admired as it was a gesture I could never make myself. "We know you're worried about the Emperor finding you, but I'll keep you safe, just like I've kept Bill safe all these years. The best thing you can do is to live quietly and try not to draw attention to yourselves."

"How am I supposed to do that when I've got green hair?" I pointed out.

"We'll think of something. Anyway, hopefully Flarp will keep the Andromedans busy and they won't have time to worry about you."

"Or how about a new hat?" Holly suggested.

"I'm not wearing your Harry Hideous baseball cap if that's what you're saying," I said firmly.

"He's just misunderstood," Holly said, patting the picture of Harry Handsome on her t-shirt.

"There is one more secret we haven't told you," Bill said, finishing his cake. He always finished first but never took a second slice, another trait I admired but would never possess.

"What is it this time? I know, Holly's from Neptune," I suggested.

Mary smiled. "No, Holly's from Birmingham. The secret is to do with you both. We love you, just as much as if you were our own children. We've done all the paperwork." Bill waved a to-do list cheerily. "Well, nearly all. And I've talked to your parents, Jasper. Everyone agrees it would be the right thing to do. The only thing left is to ask you."

Looking back I was probably being a bit thick at this point. "Ask us what?"

"You want to adopt us?" Holly said.

"We want you to think about it. You don't have to say yes right away. You don't have to say yes at all if you don't want to. You'll have a home here for as long as you wish, whatever you decide."

It wasn't the hardest decision I've ever had to make.

We said yes, of course, even though it was a bit complicated. Mary and Bill said they could be my Earth parents and Mum and Dad could be my Gloop

parents. Seemed like a good deal to me. So that's
what happened and now everything is sort of back
to normal. We even got away with being off school
all that time, as Mary told them we had had a rare
disease called *Limax Maximusitis*. I was shocked
that Mary could lie so easily but then she told me it
meant Giant Slug-itis which was true – at least for
me it was.

So, back to normal. Well, apart from having four
parents, green hair, and the right to rule a distant
planet one day. I'm proud to be from Gloop, even if
I can't tell anyone in case the Emperor of
Andromeda tracks me down and kills me. It's a
pretty good incentive to keep quiet. And Holly still
likes Harry Handsome. Actually, that reminds me…

TURNS OUT THINGS AREN'T AS NORMAL AS THEY SEEM

Being an alien and the rightful heir to the Gloop throne made me feel a bit different from my classmates at school. So finally I decided to tell them. Sort of.

"Your hair looks like snot," someone said to me in the corridor, as usual.

I was tired of thinking up witty replies. "I'm an alien," I answered, and walked off.

It felt great to tell the truth. 'Alien' even became my nickname. I was hiding in plain sight.

"I'm not bothered about being an alien any more," I said to Holly one day when I got home from school.

Holly had started letting me into her room again, just every now and then, and we would have a chat. Sometimes we wouldn't even mention Gloop. It was enough to know we'd both been there, and that one day we'd get to go back. Also we had quite a few guests these days and Mary said it was best not to say anything about Gloop or the Emperor in front of them, just in case. Our house was now on some sort of alien directory that rented out rooms on different planets and you never knew who, or what, was going to be at the breakfast table.

"I said, I'm not bothered about being an alien anymore."

"Mmm," Holly said.

"Want to know why?"

"Mmm."

"It's all about perspective. Flarp told me. Anyone not from your planet is an alien, right? But you're not from *my* planet. So you're the aliens, not me. I mean, I know this is your planet so you're not aliens now, I am, but if you came to Gloop…" I stopped.

"Hols?"

"Mmm."

That was strange. Holly hadn't told me to shove off, get stuffed or curl up and die. Maybe she was ill. Was I brave enough to touch her forehead and risk being punched in the face? I sidled up the bed towards her. She was sitting up and staring straight ahead. On the wall opposite was a new poster, bigger than any she had put up so far.

"Oh no. Not him."

It was our old friend Harry Handsome. The poster announced his new solo tour: the Follow Me tour. 'Book now for Harry's biggest ever live performance!' Crowds of teenage girls were pictured lining up behind him, their eyes fixed glassily on their hero. Harry's own eyes looked out of the poster towards us. They were large and brown, with little twinkles of light like reflections in a secret pool…

With surprising difficulty, I tore my eyes away. "Hols? Holly, wake up! Holly?"

I stood in front of the poster. Holly shook her

head as though released from a trance.

"Oh, it's you. Shove off, meat brain."

"I can't believe you still like him after all he did."

"I think we misunderstood him. He was getting rid of the Emperor to help us. He can't be evil. I mean, just look at him."

I started to, then dragged my eyes away. "No! There's something wrong with that poster. It's hypnotising you or something. Next thing you'll be booking tickets for his tour."

"Mmm."

"Holly!"

"All right, I have booked tickets! Me and Kirsty are going."

"You're mad. I've got a bad feeling about this. I am the Slime King, you know. I could order you not to go."

"I'm not one of your subjects, am I? Shut up a minute." Holly checked her phone. "Kirsty can't come."

"What are you looking at me like that for?"

"You're coming with me, amoeba face."

I glanced back at the poster – quickly, so I wouldn't get sucked in. What was Harry planning? Why was he still pretending to be a pop star – and a bad one at that? There had to be something going on, and maybe it involved Emperor Spinychops as well.

I sighed. "All right then. Maybe coming with you would be a good idea after all…"

The End… *for now.*

DID YOU KNOW...

The Andromeda Galaxy really is due to merge with the Triangulum Galaxy in about two and a half billion years.

Andromeda will also collide with the Milky Way but don't worry, we have four billion years to think of a plan.